Maggie Harris was born in Guyana and has lived in Kent and Wales. A poet and prose writer, she won the Guyana Prize for Literature in 2000 and is the Caribbean winner of the 2014 Commonwealth Short Story Prize. She has taught Creative Writing at the University of Kent and was an International Teaching Fellow at Southampton University.

What a treat is in store for readers as they discover this superb collection of eclectic stories and poems from the Guyanese writer, Maggie Harris.

Broadstairs, Margate, Ramsgate – this part of the Kent coast is a far cry from her native Guyana, but through a diverse collection of stories she paints such vivid shades of humanity.

The pull of the sea brings in refugees, families, tourists, 'cool boys', the lonely, the dispossessed, saviours, ordinary folk … all reflected in this fabulous collection.

The stories are funny, sad, moving, poignant, touching and whimsical – brilliant!

There is something for everyone in this collection – animals, families, history, humour, magic, memory, mystery, raw emotions, realism, the sea, time slips/travel and war.

I think this collection will make a fine book-group reader. I shall certainly be adding it to our collections in Southwark and Lewisham libraries. I particularly loved 'Talking Books' (so realistic) and 'When Benjamin Zephaniah came to Broadstairs'.

It is a very brave collection as Maggie Harris has obviously decided to do something quite different and exciting. I for one can't wait to see more of her splendid writing – no pressure of course.

Sandra A. Agard, Literature Development
Officer for Southwark and Lewisham Libraries

A complex love letter to the Kent coastline that Harris moved to when she was a teenager, *In Margate By Lunchtime* is an accomplished examination of displacement and discovery. Written in a vibrant prose style that – especially in its use of colour and poetic rhythm – also recalls the landscape of the author's native Guyana, these stories linger in the mind, posing difficult questions and providing unexpected answers.

John Lavin, Fiction Editor, *Wales Arts Review*

In
MARGATE
by Lunchtime

Other books by the author

Sixty Years of Loving Cane Arrow Press (2014)

Canterbury Tales on a Cockcrow Morning Cultured
Llama Publishing (2012)

Kiskadee Girl Kingston University Press (2011)

Selected Poetry 1999–2010 Guyana Classics Library,
The Caribbean Press (2011)

After a Visit to a Botanical Garden Cane Arrow Press (2010)

Co-edited with Ian Dieffenthaller
Sixty Poems for Haiti Cane Arrow Press (2010)

In
MARGATE
by Lunchtime

MAGGIE HARRIS

Cultured Llama Publishing

First published in 2015 by
Cultured Llama Publishing
11 London Road
Teynham, Sittingbourne
ME9 9QW
www.culturedllama.co.uk

A CIP record for this book is available from The British Library

ISBN 978-0-9926485-3-4

Printed in Great Britain by Lightning Source UK Ltd

Cover design by Mark Holihan
Illustration by Maggie Harris

Contents

for Ricky Wood (August 1956 – March 2014)
Let's remember you laughing, Ramsgate boy

Foreword

My very first visit to Thanet: 1972, aged 18 and new to the country. The sun is shining, Margate is jam-packed with holidaymakers. There are cool boys with long hair and blue eyes. The people I'm with are looking at properties. Next stop, Ramsgate Beach. We wander, their little girl and I, past Pleasurama, a row of seaside entertainment – dodgems, bingo callers, amusement arcade, the waltzer. My eyes are popping out. So this is the seaside! It is a far cry from Guyana, whose only beach I knew was a stretch of sand between itself and Suriname, serenaded by palm trees. In the midst of my excitement, at the smell of the salt sea, at the cacophony of music, laughter, whistles and screams coming from the helter-skelter, a deep well of loneliness colours my happiness. I know no-one here. My family are thousands of miles away, my father is recently dead, my friends are all left behind in the Caribbean sun. I am a lonesome pioneer. That is when I see them, those young people larking about on the waltzer: the boys chat me up, the girls tease me. They want to know where I came from, whether I would come to live in Ramsgate. We hang out for an hour or more. There is a lump in my throat when I have to leave.

One of the guys was called Ricky. In due time he would become my brother-in-law, gather me into the fold. In due time Thanet would become my home; I would be married, have children, go to university, become a writer. Thanet would change, the seaside lose its traditional appeal, hotels become hostels, cafés and bars change hands, the Hoverport close, the fortunes of the ferries rise and fall, property prices fluctuate. A small folk gathering in Pierremont Park would grow to become an international festival, Broadstairs Folk Week.

Thanet's outward appeal is always the sea, that bringer of marauders, tourists, seafarers and refugees; the place to sit and contemplate against its white cliffs. But there's another layer, one you only experience if you breathe the air here for more than a season: the layer of lives lived, the highs, the lows, its underclass, its dissatisfaction and pride, its artistic underbelly. There are limpets and there are floaters, constant waves of influences from those passing through and those washed in, a response to a unique environment. Newcomers keep coming and sniffing the air, being regenerated, feeling that rush of creativity inspiring them to start businesses, a better life, retire. Not all goes swimmingly; there are layers of sediments, lost hopes, broken spirits, hardened hearts damaged by disappointment and injustice. True of all places, but unlike anywhere else. Thanet's location and history make it unique, perched on the east coast, the historic city of Canterbury on its shoulder, the rolling garden county of Kent leading to that city of cities, London. The French coast, visible on clear days, keeps us apart and braces us for invasion in turn, reminds us we are at the edge of the known world. The Wantsum – that river that once made Thanet an island, encircling it from Richborough to Reculver, ushering in ships to bring war, conquest, trade – may have silted up, removing its status. But there is still a tribal gathering into itself; a recognition, which I personally hope will not disappear beneath the building over of green spaces and the closure of the airport, as these green spaces define the territories between the three main towns of Ramsgate, Broadstairs and Margate. And let's not forget the villages, those fields the Vikings trampled, where Huguenots hid in priest holes, villages that house tale upon tale, which traverse the world from Minster to Mumbai. These stories are born from my intimacy with a corner of England that became my second home, and which, through my time there, offered me my most fruitful years. They give a nod to the past, invoke time travel, allow the mystical and magical to have a voice. Of course they are not finite, stories never are.

Maggie Harris

After a Shower of Rain
a find of Roman coins in the parish of Minster

There they were, tired eyes in the dirt
Frozen tears the moon might have dropped in her passing
Some blinked at the unaccustomed light
Others hid their semi-circular selves
Nestling back into the comforting shadow.
The fingers that lifted them brushed the earth free
Years fell like the rain that had up-surged them
From a soil of roots and stones
Pre-Christian bones
Feathered strips of hide and skin.
They turned their Roman faces up to another tomorrow
Settled into the discoverer's palms
Small discs of sorrow.

I, Parakeet

They say someone left the cage door open in North-down Park in 1969, and out they flew, those incandescent birds. One comes daily, tells me tales. Some say it's only my imagination.

'If you're looking for a tale of Columbus,' he says, 'forget it. I'm no archaeologist, no Sherlock, I'm just a bird. Okay, not *just* a bird. You got other names for me, sure. Vermin. Overhead rat. We're spoken of in the same vein as seagulls, hah! Now, *those* are rats.'

I hail from the continent of magic realism, where Anansi spins tales and kiskadees corrupt the morning air, so talking birds are nothing new to me.

'Survival of the fittest,' he carries on. 'That's what it comes down to, innit? Struggle through the tough times, wade through the lean ones. Some of you harbour romantic notions, see the sea and off you go dreaming. Like me, see a flash of green and the tropics straightaway come to mind. Some, ahem, do think me beautiful. I won't argue with that. I do have a certain *je ne sais quoi*. My emerald-ness is mythic. We are the ones chosen to light up these drab skies of yours, provide a flash of effervescence.'

I pull my laptop closer, carry on with my research. He gets bold, flutters down, taps on the keys with his beak.

'Did you know we've replaced seagulls in the hatred department? They shake their fists at me from gardens and bedroom windows, walking the dog, fixing roofs, or whatever! And the language! I have to cover the young 'uns' ears sometimes. *Effing this* and *effing that*. We mystify them, see. What with all the tales and theories about where we come from, how long we've been here. Then there's the clever ones – historians, scientists, botanists … dealing in "facts". Ah, but what about the other lot, aye?'

'"Other lot?"' I ask wearily.

He shakes his head then, looks up at me, head cocked to the side.

'Think you know it all, don't you?' he states.

I have more important business to mind; I'm thinking about the centuries rolling, all those people and happenings we'll never know about. But he drags me from Romans and Vikings and smugglers.

'Think I'm just an overhead shit sprayer do ya? What you gonna write about anyway? Sailors? Dreamland? The airport? 'Oliday makers?' He flies up, lands on my dressing table and peers at himself in the mirror above the poster of Broadstairs beach.

'Where there's feathers there's tales,' he says. 'You should know. Coming from where you do, giving beads to the "natives" was what they done, weren't it?'

He flies to the window then and turns, a parting shot…

'Put me in *somewhere* at least, and me mates.'

He takes to the skies.

Bright Island

There is blood in the water. The tide washes it up on the bank. Pink foam turning to grey, scalloped like oyster shells. They call this the muddy waters. The soil will not stay still. They say elephants still trumpet here from below, singing their way home. That must have been a fine time, before this, Romans in all their finery riding on elephants through the arch at Rutupaie![1]

Much settles here, where the river bends. Iron rings. A bird's wing, still incandescent. Wedges of blackened wood. A soldier's cape. His bruised sword. The waters abandon them on their journey. Flings them at the turn of each tide. They lie like offerings to the gods.

They call this Bright Island, on account of the fires they have to light when troubles come. Trouble always comes from the sea. They call it also Tenet, Thanatos, Land of the Dead. I care nothing for names. All I want is my mother back.

---

1 Ritupaie – Roman name for Richborough

My father holds close a cup of tin carved with the mark of the eagle. It is good for tallow, and warms the hands as it glows. He tells me tales of wood and stone, flint and barges. He sweeps his hands wide to show me how once the forest had marched down to the sea. His father before him and father before *him* ferried this water. He tells again the tale of Rutupaie, the powerful arch, the stones set in times past, flint on flint, marble even. The arch stretched my neck upwards, the sky swimming; eagles paused there quite happily. As a child I thought it most powerful, and longed to vault those stones with my fingers and toes, touch the sky. I've seen those creatures that climb so, shimmying up with their elbows and knees, their screeching cries, their long tails. They come with the traders. It is said they travelled far from here. I close my eyes tight to imagine what I would see from such a height. The fort and town, busy, merchants and horses, soldiers guarding, the sea with its black demons. My father spoke to me stories told him past of hundreds passing through that arch, dressed in their finery, elephants and horses, falcons and eagles, bright birds in bamboo cages, red cloaks and swords catching the sun, sea conches blowing. Whilst some had stayed, building, layering, guarding, manning beacons, stockades, harbour and lea, others bore through and away, Durovernum, Londinium and those inner lands it is said are full of marvels and madness in equal terms, wild pagans with blue faces.

For some short years I knew no fear. My brother and I ran wild like samphire along the cliffs, rivalled the kittiwakes with our screaming. We swirled and watched the marshes spin beyond the fort, the sun race the shadows along the ditches, the fields dance their heads of corn, the dark belt of forest, the sea ram the sand below like angry goats. Ships there were always sailing the Wantsum, full of trade, circling us, to and fro Reculver, their sails pummelled by the wind.

Our eyes widened at the scan of the sea, at shapes always on the horizon. They rose at the tips of our fingers, shadows that melted away like mists. It was said some lived there on islands, rich and fertile, but which bore the brunt of wild and monstrous winds. Only the bravest sailed regularly between those angry waters which could swallow men and craft like berries.

We clambered the rocks, chased the sea's greedy fingers, gathered seaweed with our mother, wore some as crowns and veils, laughing. In the field we scattered seeds, chased the birds with our hands and voices, tying rags to poles, whispering with the wind.

She could blow a powerful fire, my mother, her cheeks as red as flames and her eyes grey as the sky. She could capture birds for the pot with stillness and her bare hands. At nights she held us close, her salty breath and breasts a cushion against the cold.

My father took my brother hunting, sometimes they would go with others, would not return for days. My mother always wore a frown on her face at these times; she did not like to see them disappear into the trees. She feared the dark, was happiest in the meadow where the sheep grazed, and in the open fields where we planted corn and she sang, as she lifted their ripe ears. But the men might return with boar, which was a feast, and always rabbits and birds, and we would share it over the fire, women, men, children, all.

There is no one time I remember fear entering my heart. It grew slowly, as we did, as days do. Men who didn't return from hunting, a fever spreading, horsemen, a child taken. News of fighting and discord at the fort. Sometimes dawn would bring the smell of smoke, and stories travelled, not only by mouth, but by horse and feather, of demons coming from the sea. Sometimes slaves escaped the fort, sought shelter in the tunnels in the chalk cliffs, we heard the dogs.

The stories of the demons were another thing. There is no word to shape the staggered beat of the heart as stories come. No way to frame the words invader, sea, smoke. Those were short years of tides I ran joyfully; too soon the thrill of shells and purses turning on the tide became something else.

That they should come for my mother. That they should come for my mother!

This river here, this river here, my father says, has more tales than there are days and nights, and around the coast, under the cliffs, the amber has absorbed more blood than there is water in the sea. His tone is bitter now.

But they wanted me. They wanted me.

No-one sees us here. It is the place they fear, where detritus settles. Here, in olden days, they called it the place of the dead. There may be no truth in it. Everywhere is the place of the dead.

Choose, they told her, laughing. We are not greedy men, we are not savages.

I have seen much dead. 'Ah, Simmi,' my father says, his head in his hand.

She let me run. Stayed.

No-one sees us here. For all their armour, those who once ran the fort were afraid of many things, river gods, ravens, old women. They went crazy if they found our offerings hanging from trees. They set fire to them, to whole trees, setting to with their torches and scorching the earth. For laughter, some of us had hung our underwear with amber beads. My father says they thought their gods the only ones. But my confusion grew, how quickly order disintegrates. I thought hourly of their fine buildings and their muddy hearts. But these are worse, these others.

Would that we had heeded my father's words!

Her arms were outstretched ushering me to run, run.

The ships that came and went these long years he had

said, return with force. Flames light the beaches as far as Dubris. Fire jumps straight out of their heads, like horns. When I was a child they had caught such a demon; even the men amongst us stood a dwelling wide away. The demon spoke a language foul as ravens, and even as they ran their knives along his throat his incantation tore the air amongst us. I myself saw the sleeping birds rise their wings and leave.

My father could do nothing for her. Her broken body bled into the earth. All night the screams and fires blazed. My brother we had no sight of.

The words my father spoke have all night swarmed my head like bees. Tomorrow, he said, we head for the trees.

Dawn

Minster Abbey, set to the torch by the Danes in 998

Dawn accompanies the Abbess across the court-yard, lighting the way as she pushes the door of the Chapel open. The Abbess's gown sweeps the stones. In the muted light she lights a candle on the wall. She kneels at the altar, makes the sign of the cross, bends her head to her palms. 'Mother of God, pray for us.' Beads of the rosary slip through her fingers: amber. Prayer by prayer drops between the folds of her gown. 'These are Christian times,' she whispers. 'Christian times.'

Dawn creeps slowly past.

The vixen slinks low along the wall, her belly swinging with cubs. She noses along the pig-sty for scraps, aware of the bodies in a pile, snoring. She crawls beneath the gate onto the farm-track. The moon picks out the brush of white, undulating.

Through the muffled light the sisters file in to pray.

Candles light their veiled heads, their clasped hands. They look towards the Abbess, drawing strength, draw close together, shoulders bowed.

She must hold the faith for the others. Her thoughts must not stray, nor thoughts of fleeing.

In the cabbage fields, dawn alights on toughened leaves crisp with frost, their small heads nestled. It accompanies the vixen along rippled rows of earth.

It reveals as it runs, brings the tale of its journey to bear on the ears of corn and wheat. Voiceless, it can only offer colour and shade, promise warmth. Its narrative lies in its ability to reveal and provoke. It bares the footprints of yesterday, the deepened print, the light disturb of soil. It circles the wooden handle of the plough, the space between, the print of the farmer's hands. It falls on a crust of bread, a rind of cheese, an apple core a sister had flung. It aids the vixen's nosing of them, her swallow. It dallies over the ditch, offers a curve along the bank, leaves the reeds to their darkness, leaves them to the winds it knew were coming, the soft bog where dragonflies still slept and creatures burrow, inhale, regurgitate, defecate.

If it could look back it would see the marshes lift into the morning like a ghostly ship with sails, the water between answer the sky, draw the thin clouds down into itself, offer them passage. It would see the fields become distinct with what they grow, frost on the leaves turn to dew and sparkle, the heads of wheat like spears, a rabbit dash between the clods of earth. It would see the sweep of the land circle the farm houses, the huddle of them into comfort, the Abbey between solid like the Father in whose name it was built. It would see a late sister scurry across the yard, fragmented sleep blur her vision; see her stumble over the stone, see the Abbess gather the sisters in prayer. *She* is not voiceless.

'Mother of God, pray for us.'

If dawn could look back it would see the line of smoke along the shore, thin wisps changing shape like clouds, billowing black. It would see them grow full with wind and fuel, race like runners abroad with lighted beacons on beach and cliff-top. It already knows the longboats that have beached themselves up on the mud and sands. Their lights preceded its own, their torches, muted on the horizon, now blaze along the beaches, the smell of burning carrying its acrid taste into the mouths of those just rising. It is this that causes the Abbess to press hard on her amber beads, knowing this time there is no time to settle the innocents onto carts, or take to horses even, for the long run to Canterbury. Even as she leads the prayer, she knows there is no time for earthly deliverance, only deliverance into the hands of the Almighty. She knows the boats across the Wantsum will be bowing beneath the weight of souls it carries, and only faith will deliver them safely across the water, blazing with the invaders from the far sea. There is no time to gather the sisters up and hide, nor seek the tunnels, nor aid the faithful inhabitants of the cottages.

But there is another reason she stands in the chapel: her word and the word of God are all she has to keep them strong, keep them believing. If she were to encourage them to run in the face of adversity, would that not weaken the very reason she was Abbess? She pushes away brief images of herself as a girl, standing at the crossroads of who she would be wife to, the Lord or that young man with the blue eyes. 'We are safe here, in the house of God,' she voices at the hopefuls who are crowding into the chapel. 'The Lord will protect us.' Her own heart is fluttering, not all these Britons believe in the true Augustine path; still the pagans practise their dark ways, a circumstance of the savage history of this country. But she is God's messenger, she must not falter.

She leads them in prayer, the rosary between her fingers, 'Hail Mary, full of grace,' pausing for the murmured reply, rippling from their bowed heads.

If dawn could look back it would see figures rise, prod the young awake, take foot with bags stuffed in panic, fowl in cages swung on shoulders, geese swept ahead with crooks across the fields. If it could look back it would see small boats across the Wantsum, paddles beating the water hard, heads looking east and west for longboats sweeping into view. If it could look back it would see those who know the tunnels seek their passages. If it could look back it would see the lovers hiding in the marshes, holding breath in through the reeds, would see the ones too slow to run seek safety in their age, sit by their hearths with eyes weary of life. It would see the devils come charging over the fields, fearing no Christian God, filled with the fury of their own circumstance, set them alight, all – thatch and wood, sty and paddock, gowns and linen, chalice and peat, Abbey and cross, men, women, children, bodies braced close rib to rib, toe to heel, breath to breath, the Abbess herself becoming like them all, ash to ash. It would see the cinders fall over the fields, follow in its wake.

If it could hear, it would hear their screams, hear prayers abandoned, hear the pound of heart and paws, the scrape of claws, the sudden silence of the vixen; the birds vacate the trees, rise upwards.

But dawn has no ears, and does not look back. It is heading west, they're awaiting it there, to do what it does, reveal and provoke.

The Shepherdess

Ursula ran laughing through the orchard. The trees were full of fruit, their gnarled branches outstretched. The dog ran beside her, his ears lifting back and forth. His head was raised to her, ready to stop when she stopped.

The sun sprinkled through the leaves. It sprayed the clearing with gold and copper. She stopped, bent to catch her breath. The dog began to nose. Apples had fallen and he had a particular liking to them.

'Don't eat too many Romeo, you'll catch colic!' Her voice rose up into the trees. An apple fell. The dog ran around her, barking. 'I know, Romeo, I know. Enough folly, let's find them then.' She looked back briefly where the rest of the flock grazed, head down in the meadow.

She took to her heels again, broke through the orchard. In the far distance the towers of Reculver commanded what had once been Wantsum's gateway to the sea. A vantage point, this high bank; not by other standards, not by the hills of Folkestone which rose up out of the land like the sleeping backs of giants; no; here a hillock barely rose above the flat fields, small undulations hedged by blackthorn and holly, hawthorn and blackberry. Clutches of elm rose in the distance, a cluster of oak edged the wood. Many had been felled, years since, for ships and houses, for countless wars, and now deer broke through to graze the edge of farmland. Sheep frequently got wedged in the clawing hedges, or broke into the orchards to nose the windfall. It was three ewes Ursula now sought. She stood still, her hand resting lightly on the dog's head. She looked down and smiled: he still carried an apple.

Her ears were pricked, listening for their cries; there was a ringleader amongst them who constantly escaped the meadow, either of a wandering spirit or sheer folly. Where she led her sisters followed.

Sandie stood by the walls of the playground, waiting. The throng had gathered: parents, carers, grandparents. Some drew on hasty cigarettes and flicked them over the wall.

She stood thin in her Superdry coat and shivered. Her hands closed on the purse in her pocket and she mentally ran over the list her mother had given her: milk, potatoes, butter, bread, beans; a fiver on the electric. She was supposed to be at college today. She thought of the others getting on with their coursework, heading into town for McDonalds. She wondered if her mother's latest boyfriend would still be home when she returned.

The siren went and the doors opened. Children broke out into the playground like schools of fish. The bright colours of their coats weaved against the grey stone, the terracotta tarmac. Her twin sisters broke out of a wave of parrotfish, skipped towards her, laden with book bags and lunchboxes, waving letters and paper crowns of coloured card. She gathered them close and headed for the Year 5 door. Her brother came out, coat unbuttoned, shirt hanging out of his trousers. He bagged her on the knee and ran off. Her shouts were lost in the wild screams released into the playground. The parakeets screamed from the nearby park.

She grasped her sisters' hands and steered them through the playground, her eyes darting ahead to fix on her brother. His ginger hair was a buoy bobbing in a swirling sea.

She ignored the glances from some of the parents, their pitying glances, their heads shaking.

Ursula held her palm above her eyes and scanned the dark edge of the neighbouring field. Would they have been foolish enough to go there? That would give her no surprise; they had already been rescued, some weeks hence, up to their knees in the bog where the river was silting up. She sighed and made her way down through the cabbages. Romeo ran ahead of her, the apple still in his mouth. At the bottom of the field she stooped, gazing at the break in the hedge. Something caught her eyes, wool, caught in the bramble.

The silly things had gone into the wood. She sighed and looked up at the sky. It was an hour yet until the sun fell. She would give it no more time than that. She stamped on the broken hedge and entered the trees. The birds were getting ready to roost; she had learnt their soft burrs, their sleep cries. All her life, knew them from the vigour of mornings. Some of them liked to keep moving until all daylight was gone, hugging the branches and kitchen gardens, dipping across the fields. They frequently had stones thrown at them, by the old, disgruntled and ready for sleep, and by the young for mischief.

There was no path here, just staggered tracks from the deer or the occasional huntsman. Sometimes, at blackberrying, Ursula and the village children would wander at the fringes of the wood, daring each to venture deeper. But such were the tales that filled their heads, of sorcerers and ghosts, that not many entered, not least because of the sightings still of wild boar. One had killed a man from Stourmouth just a month since, he had set off in high spirits with sticks and knives and rope like a medieval. They said the creature had bore down on him with a wild and sudden rage. She kept her glances wary now, listened carefully, even as each step she herself took cracked twigs this way and that. Overhead, the branches of larch and birch whispered. There was a yew centred hereabouts, she recalled, she had gazed on it as a child, a wondrous thing, full of magic. Some had hung wishes on it that time, praying for the king to be restored to his rightful place. Her uncle was one who had boasted loud and foolishly, and lived to do so no longer, marching with the Medway men and never returning.

'Shoo Romeo!'

She stood still, lifted her head.

They were pleading to go to the park. The girls' faces turned up, their eyes grey like the sky, her brother already ahead, running. Sandie hesitated. What was the harm? Whatever she did wouldn't be right. She thought of the stares in the playground, knew their pity stemmed from the role she had been forced into. 'Poor lamb,' she had heard one whisper.

'Ten minutes is all,' she said.

They turned down the alley past the school. The path was muddy and pitted with dog turds. The Clean Up signs rusted on the sagging wire fence. The backs of houses leaned into the alley. Washing hung from plastic lines. Who'd have thought this was all fields once, she thought, a brief snatch of a history lesson returning, one of the few she had caught. A man coughed behind a fence. Her brother was away and onto the grass, heading for the climbing frame. He was a chimpanzee swinging, book bag a red splash on the wood chippings. Sandie walked over and picked it up, settling it with the others on the bench. She sat back and lit a cigarette, watching her sisters crawl up the slide the wrong way. She thought of the rips in the knees of their tights but said nothing; she lifted her eyes to the trees, drawing the smoke down into her lungs.

Light was a muted spray through the leaves. Ursula could see no further evidence of the ewes' passage. She stood still, unsure how far to venture.

Romeo sat back, his ears back. He dropped the apple.

Suddenly, he dashed forward, plunging ahead through bracken and a mound of fallen logs. Ursula called his name once, sharply.

He didn't return. She could hear the splintering of twigs and his heavy crashing about. He had no finery, did Romeo. She heard him bark, loud and incessant. It was his rounding-up bark. She tried to follow him on hands and knees.

'Come on you lot! It's time to go!' Sandie gathered up the bags and headed for the alley. Her sisters came behind her, protesting.

She shouted her brother's name, looked back. He was nowhere to be seen.

She ran her eyes swiftly across the park, the climbing frame, the swings, and roundabout. The park was emptying. There was no sign of a carrot head.

'Where's Ryan? Did he go off somewhere?'

Her sisters shook their heads. As always, they were only concerned with each other.

'Flipping heck! I only took my eyes off him for a minute! Are you sure you didn't see him head off? Last time I looked he was on the tyres!'

They shook their heads, looking up at her with their stone-grey eyes.

'Stand here and don't move,' she said. She dropped the bags at their feet and walked round the swings. There was a solitary elm here, a good hiding place. She bet he was bloody larking about. She circled it and looked up into its thick branches. Her upturned face was pale and tight with anger.

'Ryan! RYAN! Are you up there? Stop playing silly buggers, we've got to go!'

She caused a disturbance; some of the parakeets screeched down at her.

'RYAN!'

Romeo was clawing under the fallen logs, his nose edging the earth beneath. Ursula crouched down and peered beneath the logs. She could see nothing but darkness. The ground was soft and she felt it fall away beneath her fingers. She paused. The dog pushed past her and disappeared.

'Careful Romeo!'

She sat back and waited. He was good with sheep, Romeo was. If they'd fallen somewhere he'd soon nose them out.

Sandie was making herself hoarse shouting his name.

'Ryan!'

She looked back at the entrance to the alleyway. The twins were silhouetted against the fence, their hoods up. From here they looked like crows. She shivered. It was getting dark. Behind them the clouds were spinning past.

Ursula heard a sheep cry then, to her left. She stood up and peered through the darkening shadows falling vertically between the tree trunks. Ivy cut diamonds between branch and leaves. Aerial roots were becoming limbs and claws. Spiders' webs caught the dying light, glistened. The cry came again and she followed it. Two stood there, grey like twilight, motionless and unbothered, their coats a rack of bracken and twigs. In the shadows they looked like fanciful creatures, dragons or some such. She shivered.

'You foolish things! Where's your sister?'

They looked up at her blankly and began to make their way past her.

She waved, trying to still them.

'Wait!'

They ignored her, carried on.

She looked round.

'Romeo! Here boy!' She whistled.

There was no answering bark.

The shadows were creeping more thickly now. She would have to leave the other until the morrow. Common sense told her the two were making their way back, retracing their steps out into the fields. But Romeo did not answer.

She went back to the pile of fallen logs, fell to her knees again, peered beneath, and called his name, over and over again.

'RYAN!' It was no good; she had skirted the playground, peered into every hiding place she considered possible, from litterbins to the boarded-up toilet block, behind the fence to the thin spaces between the alleyway and the backs of the houses, the school grounds.

Her sisters walked ahead of her, their heads together. From somewhere a dog appeared between them and they took it in turns to run their hands over his head. He was covered in earth and leaves and looked about him this way and that, jumped at a car hooting. Sandie was too angry with Ryan to fret about it, they were always begging for kittens and hamsters, rabbits and puppies. She caught up with them as they approached the traffic lights.

'Did you two really not see Ryan go? You must've!'

They shrugged and shook their heads. 'Well you wait

till I get hold of him! I'll bloody kill him.'

She forgot about the shop and the purse hanging heavy in her pocket, only steeled herself for her mother's angry face rising up from the sofa. The lights turned green and she grabbed their hands, shepherding them across the road. The dog followed.

In Margate by Lunchtime

Silas paused from raking the seaweed to watch the hoy come in. She had dropped her sails and was almost inshore, moving slowly and turgidly through the water. Beyond her, sails sketched the horizon. He spat the stench from his throat. They'd be in The Watermen's Arms tonight, the crew, drinking their salt cares away. His business was to be there too.

He turned and headed back up the cliff. It was testing land, running straight to the cliff edge, frilled with vetch and samphire. He'd lost too many sheep, fence or no fence. He just kept two ewes now, close to the cottage. Around him cornfields stretched, the windmill in between, the church and manor estates filling his vision. In the distance, the Reculver towers stood sentinel over a river that was no more. The place reeked with ghosts; he had no time for it. He looked back, and watched the hoy close the gap between the pier head. It was but a mile or so from here, but he could imagine the passengers climbing all relieved, their bags close, their legs weak, their bellies lurching from the suffering borne through the buffering winds. His thoughts wandered on them. Come to take the air? Talk business? There'd be rich pickings amongst them he was sure.

He mopped up Lizzie's nettle broth with bread and left the cottage, crossed Marsh Bay. Light was fading, but there was a moon hanging, lighting his way into Margate. His steps took him past the Infirmary, the inmates all gathered in, pulled out from the blessed air with their shawls wrapped round their knees, gas lamps flickering in the windows. Past the Nayland Rock, and the new houses just built, Buenos Aires. Buenos bloody Aires. What a name for dwellings meant to live in. Silas could make no sense of those who plundered other lands and brought their strangeness back. What for?

The moonlight caught the frill of the waves as they sighed on the sand, foamed and fell back. The bathing machines lay silent, no sound of laughter and splashing coming from them now; these new people come to take the air were most likely tucking into ale and pots of beef in the hostelries. Silas could imagine the talk, listening was his business, and talk now was full of the air and opportunity. He wondered briefly on the women getting ready for bed, their curled hair and bonnets, high-bodied dresses and shawls. He could imagine linen and silk as he had stroked them between his own fisher-fingers one night at Kingsgate when the French ship had come aground. It was luck then, and a fair amount of planning. Even some that went a-foying had grease on their fingers. They watched the weather, read the wind, knew that the naval press gangs were busy at Cliffsend, swung the light, lured them in like herrings. He thought of the barrels hidden in the tunnels beneath the very earth he walked on. He would have liked to have kept a roll of silk for Lizzie. Could just imagine her eyes shining as she draped it round her still-fine shoulders. But there were those who had more occasion to wear silk than his Lizzie, whose day was spent raking and weeding, gathering and boiling. But not much longer if he could help it.

A carriage and four clattered past him, spitting dust and stones as it sped on its way. Inside, Silas glimpsed dark suits and top hats, shawls on shoulders.

The harbour-side was alive with noise and light. The oyster sellers shouted in the light of the braziers. Oranges glowed on a night stall. Lights swung from the pier and the ships alongside. A dray cart unloaded barrels of ale.

By the look and sound of it, The Watermen's Arms was doing good business. One man, crew by the look of him, was taking a piss in the gutter. Through the open door, hearty laughter and a fiddler picking up a tune. He pushed his way through.

'Silas.' Ned raised his mug from his usual stool by the bar, shifting his knees. His parrot Mary walked along the bar.

'Lively in 'ere tonight.'

'Ay, there's a few young 'uns off the boat.'

Silas looked over the heads, the bar centred like a holy grail, men gathered round. Some rough, some tidy, some hatted, some not. The windows held the night. Light flickered from oil lamps hung from the beams. At a table beneath the timbers a heated discussion was going on. Their legs were clad in long trousers and pointed collars lay flat from their necks. The African reached between them to gather the tankards.

'The hoys are finished! Finished, I say!'

'You're wrong, damn you! You're breeding disaster if you're right.'

'Think on it, man! Twenty-eight hours to voyage round the coast? What say you to news of the new steamboats then? Did you not read reports published of just eight hours, London to Margate! How can you argue with that?'

'I do not for a minute believe that! Give me proof!'

Silas turned to Ned. 'What they arguing about so strong, Ned?'

'I gather it's news of boats powered by steam to replace the hoys. Would ye believe it?'

'Tomfoolery! And steal the living from honest men?'

Ned shrugged and laughed. 'We who don't read have to await the evidence of our own eyes, Silas! Mary will tell us all, won'tcha Mary?' He tickled his parrot under the chin as she leaned in to sip from his ale. 'Right now I'm more concerned for another pint!'

Silas's ears were open and listening. Listening was his main job, equal to farming, equal to fishing for whiting or herring or mackerel, equal to knowing of tunnels and trade.

'Mark my words, within a few years not a hoy will be employed, I wager!'

Silas refused to believe the talk. If hoys were to make way for steamboats, were all sailing ships also to be abandoned? Never!

One of the London men, nay *boys*, was opening papers for display on the table.

'Read this Bertie, and tell me what it says!' He jabbed at the paper with fingers fluted with a white cuff.

'The Way Forward, Full Steam Ahead, license set to be granted ...'

The man called Bertie shook his head, disbelieving.

'Well blow me down, Charlie! So it's set to happen!'

'And happen soon, by the sound of it!'

'You know what this means, don't you?'

'Know? You think me a fool man? For sure, this my father will be keen to know!'

'Happen he might know already?! Why do you think he was so keen to set up this journey whilst we were all set for Paris?'

Bertie sat back and looked at him, wiping the froth from his lips. He shook his head slowly, a movement that soon turned to nodding. 'By bledy Jove! Charlie, you might well be right on this! I wondered what possible interest the old fool might have in Margate! There was me thinking he just set me on a wild goose chase to stop our trip to Paris – we all know what he thinks on the French! Blow me if he *planned* to divert our folly here!'

'Happen he's not such an old fool like you think he is!'

'So all that talk about seeking possible trade was a red herring … well this place is certainly rife with herrings!'

The two laughed, and Silas felt the beer in his belly roll like the old smack he shared with Ned. He couldn't tell if it was the news that bothered him or the lingering snigger in the words *herring* and *Margate*.

A week later, on the open sea past Sheerness, Silas wondered what he had let himself in for.

The young fool, Bertie Marshmount, rolled out of the cabin and stumbled an unsteady passage upwards. His hand grasped the rail, his legs wobbled. On deck, the cold wind hit him in his face, whipping his breath and tossing it into the affray. He reached out for the rail with both hands, taking what breaths he could.

'All right, Mr Marshmount?'

Silas shouted over from the wheel. The hood of his sou'wester almost covered his features and his tall dark figure cut a menacing silhouette. He seemed unbothered by the wild weather, the six foot waves rolling the small craft, which Bertie warranted listed at 40 degrees.

The wind stole his reply. Silas held the wheel fast; he had borne many a passage like this one, and was not a man to turn work away. Although, that said, he did not normally undertake such whimsical and useless employment.

Bertie's stomach was raw. Many an ale-filled night had seen him spewing up and fevered the next day. The passage on the hoy last week had been bad enough, catching them sideways all the night from Billingsgate, but she had held steadfast. This boat was an unsteady raft on an ocean. What weakness and stupidity had made him agree to a race with Charlie, even now sound and safe on land, having a wild time whipping along the Canterbury Road from Rochester? And what foolishness had decided him to risk his very life on a craft like this, poorly rigged and listing even in a flat wind, instead of doing the normal journey by hoy? Were they not setting out to prove how necessary the hoys themselves were? Or, looking forward to modern approaches, how unnecessary? Blow me, if he knew the reason and point of it, the combination of drink and Charlie were sometimes too much for the nerves.

His stomach heaved and his head bent over the side, his face straight into the devil of a wave that soaked him body and soul. His hands tightened on the boat. *O Father,* he thought, never again will I allow foolishness to guide me. Charlie *Bastardface* if I never see you again it will be too soon. He crawled his way back into the relative cocoon of the wheelhouse.

'How much longer?' he croaked.

Silas didn't reply immediately. For him time did not exist in a finite and precise manner. But he was aware that the young man beside him, white as a Whitstable oyster shell, was a creature apart. As such he deserved some answer. 'Well … we've been abroad an hour since sunrise from Rochester, and there's Sheppey we've just turned; the wind the way she's blowing is a-playing with us, she's a cat see, holding us one minute, letting us run the next. Then there's the tide, she'll be on the turn by noon, then after that, we'll just have to see.'

'Mid-afternoon then?' Bertie's face got even whiter.

'Like I said.'

'Well it is no use then, I have already lost.'

Away on the Medway shore, rich with shipping and foreign with heels and wings, Charlie paced the yard of the staging post at Rochester. He paid no mind to the tavern or the birds, or to sailing ships loaded with tales of India men or freed black men or estates to be had in the Indies. He was just waiting for a ride, a coach and four to be precise. Just his luck, just his damned, God-cursed luck; the string of misfortune. He should have been well away to Canterbury on the midnight mail coach by now. Mishap after mishap. Rain, wind and mud. The coach losing a wheel. The driver taking the mail and carrying on by horseback. Passengers abandoned. The fool of another driver had not appeared. A jolly Charlie, wide-eyed and full of high spirits en route to Rochester, now left high and dry. A gloomy sun was up already across the Medway and a stink arose from the river, sewage and oil. There was much to and froing, talk about the unreliability of the driver, already on his last warning. That did nothing to appease Charlie; he needed to be gone, or Bertie would win the wager. That could not be; whose idea was it anyway? Charlie had much to lose, his entire tuition fee for this term. What would his father say if he knew? Christ!

There were a few passengers waiting, but none as agitated as Charlie. They were a Jew and his wife, abandoned like him with the broken mail coach; a vicar, recently woken from the poor room at the back of the inn, and a German, fat and beaming, carrying a notebook which he wrote in from time to time as he stuffed his face with pie and ale. Charlie looked out into the road ahead, stretching muddied past the warehouses into the distance. Behind him both laughter and curses poured out of the open door.

'Sir. Sir!' The stable boy called out over the yard. 'Driver's here, Sir!'

Charlie's boots scraped the cobbles. A driver had appeared

from another direction, walking unsteadily towards the stables where the boy waited with a new coach and four, three grey mares and a black stallion, all tetchy and tossing their heads. It was still lashing with rain. God, what journey was he in for? He spared a thought for Bertie then, out on the devilish channel.

He gathered his bag and climbed in at the boy's nod. The vicar stood aside to let the Jewish couple alight, then folded his long thin frame into the coach, his robe sweeping the floor. There was no sign of the German. There was no waiting. The driver whipped the reins into the air and off they went, the wheels clattering across the cobbles and out into the road, the river at their back, through the outskirts of Rochester and onto the old Roman road. The countryside swum through the misted windows of the coach: high hedgerows and oak trees, farmland of barley and wheat, rooftops of farmhouses. The coach, unfortunately not one of those newly sprung, lurched on the rutted road.

Charlie closed his eyes and pulled his college scarf close; it was cold, and his coat was wet. The smell of dank wet clothing and sour breath rose from the other passengers. He wished for a sprinkle of his cologne but thought he might cause offence. He wished he were up on the box with the driver, in the fresh air, rain or no rain. He had had no sleep, but didn't expect any. Beneath his wavering lashes, he examined the feet of the priest. Sandals. In this weather. Madness. He had heard they walked the Pilgrims' Way like Franciscans. Charlie had no time for pilgrimages and priests; he dreamed of science and drawing, clean buildings with function and light.

Suddenly, the coach tilted forward and the Jewish woman catapulted against him. Flustered, he sat upright, she let out a little yelp, pulled back, hand on mouth, apologised. The coach stopped. God, what now.

He pushed the door open. The driver was on the road,

a coach wheel in a rut.

'Would you like some help there?'

'No, Sir. Fine we are.'

He guided the horses as he spoke, and the coach lurched, righting itself. Charlie shut the door. They were off again.

The Jewish woman and her husband were chattering away in Hebrew. The priest looked across at Charlie.

'The Lord will prevail,' he said.

Charlie could not bring himself to answer. Hours lost, the wager too, whose tomfool idea was this? He thought back to the night in The Watermen's Arms. That was a place to take your life in your hands. It was only bravado and ale that had furled both him and Bertie that night, spewing what they knew of London talk. Their fathers had sent them to Margate to seek out the possibility of business; what with passengers by their hundreds taking the hoys for the air, the town it seemed was ripe. Hostelries opening up, merchants bringing London fare, a library, dancing, a theatre even! But what did he and Bertie do? Get so drunk that before they knew it, one line of argument had become a plan: 'Road's the way Bertie! Boat or no boat, you mark my words!'

'Nonsense! You witless fool! Do you think this country was made great by road travel?'

'Damn it, man! Of course! The Romans could hardly sail across this country surely? Look to the evidence, all roads lead to Rome, they say!'

'I give you they did well with their straight roads and their walls but they still had to brave the waters, you fool, as do our ships now from Southampton, the Indies, India!'

'I still maintain the way forward for this country and its business is by road: no steamboat, fiction or true will spoil that!'

'And I say not!' Charlie remembered banging his fist down on the table, scattering the papers and upsetting a tankard. But both of them being so foolishly het up neither noticed. The next words had hatched the plan: a race, London to Margate one by sail, the other by road. By lunchtime, wind or no wind, horse or neigh. On the table one hundred pounds, plus lunch.

It was Silas with his ear to opportunity who brought the plan further, offering his boat, sea-ready and windsharpened. He was not so foolish as to quote evidence of endurance and run-ins with slipping naval vessels or even French patrols, but with the pub's regulars – including the landlord and Ned and nodded to by Mary – to back the sea-worthiness of The Evening Star; before they knew it dates were set, prices agreed, and now, the plan engaged.

There was a hoy ahead of them, sails at full mast. Bertie wished he was on it. He had come on deck again, finding below with its dark confinement and heaving sides more than he could bear. His imagination was taking him over. He had taken fright of wings brushing past him in the dark and a wild screech to combat the howl of the wind. He felt too much of a fool to venture forth such information to the sharp-nosed figure in the wheelhouse.

He watched the ship lean into the wind, noting for the first time how low she sailed in the water. Feeling his stomach lurch like a child in his belly, he began to wonder if perhaps Charlie was right, and road the better way after all. Bertie had never travelled the Kent stage, having heard so many reports of highway robbers, women even! Two had been hung just a year hence, an infamous gang that operated on the road to Dover. But how much safer was he here with this wizened fellow, staring motionless at the sea, in sou'westers and a cap of leather? Who would know if he decided to throw Bertie overboard, and deny all knowledge of him thereafter? More able passengers than he had lost their lives in foolish 'accidents.'

As the thought entered his head and took hold, he felt

the chap's eyes swerve on him, cold grey eyes like a fish. Bertie leaned back nervously, feeling the wedge of the boat hard up against him. There was nowhere to run. He had the money on him too, one hundred and fifty pounds: £100 for the wager and £50 for Silas. Plus, obsessed as he was with timing, his grandfather's gold watch, tucked away in his waistcoat pocket. Bertie knew that £50 was a huge sum of money for a fisherman. He looked in the hold of the boat, could find no evidence that any fish had breathed their last there … just ropes and an old iron chest. O Lord…!

'Wind's dropping.'

The words took a while to enter Bertie's consciousness, overwhelmed as his fears had been. 'What? Oh…Oh! Really? Yes I do believe you're right there.' He let out a nervous laugh. 'Does that mean we're making good time?'

'Be there in an hour I guess.'

Bertie's sigh of relief was audible. What could he have been thinking, the man was … well, just a man really, doing his job, hard life, spent on a boat like this, trying to make a living. He laughed, then attempted to turn it into a cough.

Silas tried not to take the foolishness of the idiot next to him seriously. He couldn't help being soft, that's what city life did, he saw it all the time, rich toppers from London strolling along the sea at Margate, head up sniffing the air and examining the cliffs. For a moment Silas had been tempted to throw him overboard.

At last, despite the surly driver, they made it to Canterbury; there a new coach and four waited, tossing their proud heads into the air. The priest left them, lowering his sandaled feet onto wet cobbles and drawing the sign of the cross into the air, blessed them all in the name of the Lord. The new coach was well sprung, and Charlie sat back for the last leg of the journey, still accompanied by the Jews and a merchant from Canterbury. A flattened patch of road teased them into an easier journey, but this belief soon passed, the ruts and holes returning, if less jarring due to the coach; and Charlie was relieved to see the towers of Reculver come into view. The sky was still grey, and from a distance the sea smudged the same. He could not see clearly whether there were ships out there, certainly not enough to see the little craft on which poor Bertie was almost certainly still suffering.

There was gathering at the pier, a crowd forming. The husbands' boat – so called after the men who worked in London during the week, returning to wives in Margate at the weekend – was due in shortly, and all the riff-raff was gathered, ready with their booing and cat calls littered with lusty language. The weekday wives, waiting, did their best to ignore what had become a circus, the Margatonians versus all comers, laughing them off the boats in their finery. The Bellman was there with his bell listening out for news to carry. Gentlemen's tall hats and ladies' decorated bonnets, peanut sellers, small boys darting in-between alert with eyes and fingers. Children hung close to their mother's skirts, peered out into the crowd. Charlie leapt out of the coach, come to rest by the Customs House. A hoy was in. Charlie's neck stretched above the heads all like turkeys looking beyond. His heart rapped furiously in his chest. Bertie. Where was Bertie?

He heard shouts. The crowd parted by the steps. The head of Silas appeared. Charlie elbowed his way through, his words blustering.

The sight before him caused his heart to falter. There was Bertie being brought up in a litter, his face pale as a shroud. Charlie shouted his name. The litter appeared on the quayside, was set down. Charlie leaned over him. 'Bertie! Bertie!' He looked up at Silas. 'What has happened? What have you done with him?'

'He be fine, fool just fainted. Some nonsense about a bird speaking in the wheelhouse.'

Bertie's eyelids began to flicker, then opened. Charlie caught a strong whiff of brandy.

'Charlie, did you see him, did you see him?'

'See what, you fool?'

'The India parrot, talking he was, said *Margate's the place, Margate's the place!* He lifted Gramps' watch clean out my waistcoat pocket!'

'You're raving you bledy idiot. I told you keep off the drink. Here, get up!'

'Does that mean you've won, you conniving fellow?' He sat up. Hiccupped. The crowd drew back, laughing.

Charlie helped him up, watched him pat his pockets. 'Let's call it quits, Bertie, eh? Way past lunchtime anyroad.'

'I've had an idea,' Charlie offered, as they lurched along the pier. 'It has to do with leather, and comfort.'

'Well, blow me down if I wasn't thinking similar. Got enough for a tankard?'

Lizzie was waiting for Silas by the track. Her hem was muddied, her features calm. The bird sat patiently on her shoulder.

'All went well then?' She smiled.

'Aye.' He held out his hand, unrolled the pound notes, and laid them in her hand. In his pocket the watch ticked, silent, close to his heart.

Scamp

'No-one thinks about the birds during wartime. Can't blame them really. No-one thinks about the cats and dogs neither, 'cept when it comes to eat them in times of need. It's a little-known fact that folks were instructed to have their pets put to sleep during the war. No food fer 'em, see.'

Hilary watched her grandad potter round the aviary, whispering to his pigeons, cleaning out their pens.

'I don't believe you, Grandad.'

'Well, 'tis true. Ask yer Gran. Cried buckets she did when they had to get rid of her own moggy. Seven she was.'

'Who was seven? Granny or the cat?'

Her grandad paused. 'You know, I can't remember. One of them was.'

'Well that's mean. Did you have a pet that had to be put to sleep? That's a fib anyway, they don't sleep, they die.'

'Eh. Well, yes and no.'

'Grandad! Yes or no?'

'Well …'

Hilary swung her legs from the old stool she was perching on and waited. Grandad was putting a new clip on Blueboy's leg. He'd come back from France battered and tattered, Grandad had said, and blamed those Frenchies for tinkering with him. As she watched, Blueboy cooed, and half-closed his eyes.

'I had a little Yorkshire terrier. Well, was me Nan's really …'

'She must have been really old …'

'Yeah, we're all old now, Princess. I used to tek him for walks, down the harbour and that, y'know. We had a bond, me and Scamp. Scamp his name was, yeah. Then when they said all that about the putting him to sleep I couldn't have that.'

He stopped stroking Blueboy's feathers and stared out over the allotments.

Grandad's house was called Crow Hill Cottage. It had a high garden from where you could see the sea. From up here you could see the tops of the houses and the narrow road running down to the harbour.

'No, I couldn't have that,' he said after a while. 'So I took him fer a walk see, a very long walk. One Sunday it was, only day free from doing this and that. Walked him all along the beach, past Ramsgate, as far as Cliffsend. I'd not really thought about the war much before that, what it meant. We'd seen the boys in their uniforms of course, and then there was Dunkirk, all them little ships going to bring our boys back. My Dad helped with that, him being a fisherman, sailing there and back dunno how many times. 'E could tell you a tale or two 'bout all them boys crying and dying and glad to be coming 'ome. The talk was all about 'itler, bloody 'itler, and pulling our socks up. But then things started to change, food getting less and less.' He paused and looked far away again.

Hilary waited and looked out into the distance too. It was a brilliant blue day, with tiny triangles of sail moving quickly. She'd heard Gran say something about a race and people with more money than sense.

Whilst she waited for Grandad to carry on, she thought about not having enough food. Imagine having to get rid of your pets. She'd gone without supper sometimes, when she'd been poorly, and there were times when Mum would run out of milk so they couldn't have cereal. And she was always hungry when she came home from school, but...

'I took 'im as far as Cliffsend, I did. Couldn't walk no more, thinking about the coming back and all. Told him sit on the beach and wait. I'd taken a biscuit fer him, left it on a rock nearby. I'd taught him to sit and stay, see, so I knew he wouldn't follow me. Then I left him.'

Hilary's chin slipped off her fingers.

Grandad's voice was croaky as he went on.

'I didn't look back, couldn't look back. But then something happened that took my mind off him. It was the noise. Couldn't describe it. Coming from the sky.'

He lifted Blueboy up and held him close to his old grey jumper.

'It was roaring and crackling and everything all in one. Like all the world's fireworks going off at once. You never heard a racket like it. Then the bombs started falling and I watched them drop all along the coastline, turning in on the houses, Ramsgate, Broadstairs ... I ran and ran, the sirens were going mad, and people was running for the shelters in them tunnels, and the smoke made the sky go black, you know how it looks when they're burning tyres at Manston airfield...? And I stood at the top of our road and couldn't see nothing but smoke and rubble. Nan's house was gone, just a pile of bricks.'

'Oh, Grandad ...'

'Yes, well ... we was lucky we was. Nan had popped out, gone to see someone streets away. It was only a house.

Some people lost folks. And if it wasn't for Scamp, well...'

'Did he come after you? Did you go back looking for him?'

He shook his head, and smoothed Blueboy's feathers.

'No. Couldn't. We was too occupied, sorting out Nan coming to live wi' us. And more bombs. And clearing up. And surviving. Things got tough after that. Yeah ... but I like to think he saved me life, though, and that he looked after himself catching rabbits and whatnot. Mebbe found a good 'ome on a farm or something. He was a good dog. Taught him to sit and stay I did. But I couldn't have one after. Prefer birds, they got wings, they could always fly away if they had to.'

He set Blueboy up on the perch. 'Right then ... that's enough of that. Let's go see what Gran's doing for tea. There we go now, there we go.'

The Smack Boy

'How many times have I told you to be back by six?' Danny crouched down, instinctively flinging his arms upwards to protect his head.

The man's tone softened. 'Danny, get up, you silly boy. What do you think I'm going to do, hit you or something?'

The boy peeped up at him through his fingers, his eyes flickering. 'Come, sit.' He gestured at the kitchen table.

'I was just worried,' he said, over the sound of the tap running, the kettle filling. 'You know it's only a trial, this. They'd soon take you off me if anything goes wrong.' He set two mugs down on the table.

He pulled a chair out for Danny and pushed the biscuit tin over. 'Here have one; it won't spoil your tea. You must tell me where you're going. And come back when I say. I'm not being heavy, mate, it's just house rules, innit?'

The boy mumbled.

'Sorry? Didn't hear you.'

'Lost, I got lost.'

'Lost?' Patrick threw his head back and laughed. 'How could you get lost in Ramsgate?' He pointed out the window. 'High Street. Harbour Street. Sea. You can't get lost! Not unless you go off wandering.'

Danny said nothing. That's just what he did do. Wandered. But he couldn't tell the man that. His eyes wandered to the biscuit tin. It had a picture of a ship on it, with sails.

'Here, have another," Patrick said. 'Don't worry. I'm not gonna quiz you. I bet you had enough of that in your other place.' He reached into his jacket hanging on the back of the chair.

'Here, that's for you.' He set a mobile phone down in front of Danny.

The boy was waiting for Danny on the Western Undercliff. The summer was coming to an end, and visitors were already dying away. He worried what September would bring. The boy had the same clothes on as yesterday and the day before, a loose linen shirt and rough ragged trousers. He wore no shoes.

Danny took the phone out of his pocket and showed it to him. He watched him turn it over and over in his palm, prodding it with thumbnails split and stained. His brown hair fell over his eyes like a bird's wing. 'What is it?' the boy asked.

'It's a mobile phone.'

'Phone?' He slid his fingers over the front, then shook it and held it to his ear.

Danny remembered he knew nothing. He didn't know how to explain a phone to someone who'd never seen one. He couldn't even demonstrate its use; you needed two for that. He didn't know how to explain anything to anyone no more. This place, this place of sea and ships, little passageways and row after row of houses – how different was it gonna be to all the other places they'd put him?

The seagulls screamed overhead.

'Wait,' he said, and clambered off over the rocks. There was enough rubbish on the beach to build a spaceship. He remembered his mother saying that. He found two tin cans and a length of fishermen's rope. But it didn't work. The boy looked at him strangely as he tied the ends and proceeded to speak into one and put his ear to the other.

Then, of course ... the ringtones. The boy jumped as Danny flipped his way through Drum and Bass to Placido. He tried to go on YouTube then, but there was no reception.

'Don't matter,' he said, pushing the phone in his pocket. 'Do you want to show me the tunnels now?'

The boy looked peeved. He looked out to sea then back at Danny.

'Ye got anythink else?'

Danny felt in his pocket. There was a Mars bar there, from yesterday, squashed. The boy took it from him quickly, ripping the wrapping and biting into it.

'Chocolate,' Danny said helpfully.

'I know what chocolate is,' he said. 'I'm not stupid, only dead.'

'Can you show me the tunnels now?'

'Don't ye want to see where I live first? Where do ye live?' He licked the last of the wrapper clean. Chocolate ringed his mouth. Danny pointed towards the town. The wrapper floated to the ground, the shape of the chocolate still in it. 'Oh I can't go past the harbour,' the boy said, 'Got to stay this side, see.'

'Why?'

'S'not allowed, is it?! Don't you have all the busybodies telling ye what ye can't do?'

Danny nodded, thinking back to the other place, the place he'd run away from. 'Right y'are, come along then.'

The boy set off towards the marina, keeping close to the cliff. He seemed impervious to anything else anyone else was doing. There were women and pushchairs, kids on bikes, a young girl in a wheelchair, an old geezer with a dog who cocked his leg every few steps. The boats and their moorings played music in the background.

He pushed open the door to the Sailors' Church. There was another door inside, the smell of wood, polish, candles. To the left a staircase ran upwards, up and up. Danny followed the boy's soundless footsteps, his own trainers stomping on the bare wood. Light flowed through the arched windows, the cliff loomed outside.

'Hell of a clatter wi' us all making our way up and down 'ere,' the boy said. 'Never mind the Vicar and the old bag threatening and bringing the fear of God down. I can hear them now, I can.' He laughed, and the air got colder the higher they climbed, four floors in all, till they came to the end. He paused on the landing and pushed the door open.

The sea swum through the open windows. Danny felt giddy for a bit.

The beds were all set out in a row facing the window. There was a thin grey blanket covering each, no pillow. A wooden box sat beside each bed. He wandered over and looked, a linen shirt neatly folded, a tin, a length of rope. He walked along the row looking. They were all the same. He thought of the room he'd shared back at the home, the shelves with books and Lego, the chest with spare clothes, the one poster each they'd been allowed on the wall. Then he remembered his roommates fighting, ripping his Transformers poster, stamping on the Lego garage. He looked across at the boy now, sitting on one of the beds, legs folded. His mouth was ringed with chocolate.

'Where's the others?' He asked.

The boy shrugged, he was whittling at a piece of wood with a small razor. The razor glowed between his fingers with a translucent blue. Light drained through the windows and ran along the rough floorboards, raising the cracks and splinters, coming to rest in corners, below the metal-framed beds.

'Is it just you here?'

The boy swung his legs over the bed and crossed the room. He leaned on the window-sill and looked at Danny.

'Ye ask too many questions, ye do. Questions only cause trouble, don't ye know. Ye have to do what ye're told, see. Only the Almighty knows the answer.' He looked out over the harbour, the light catching the whites of his eyes. As Danny watched, they grew wider and swum with small needles of light. He felt as if he was in one of those aquariums where tiny tropical fish darted about.

'Why did you live here, didn't you have a mum and dad?'

The boy banged his fist on the windowsill. 'I told ye! No questions!' He spun round and looked Danny straight in the eyes. 'Where be yer folks? Why are ye wandering alone? Have ye been sent to get me?'

Danny stood back from him, confused. 'Get you? What you on about? I told you when we met, I ain't got no folks. I'm newly come to this place.'

'Oh.' The boy drew back. 'Sorry, ye never know who's come to get ye, see. Some play nice, warm to ye, promise ye a pint at the Castle, promise to buy ye out, offer a proper family.' He looked out again at the harbour with its moored boats shifting on the slight sea. His tone grew lower, like the wind dropping. 'See it out there now, ye wouldn't know. Ye wouldn't know its bucking and biting, the cold whipping at ye through yer bones, yer fingers froze and bleeding grasping the nets. Ye'd believe anything, knowing.'

He turned and pointed at the empty beds one by one.

'There's Tommy, age nine, went overboard at Foreness Point. Next to him, Saul, ten year old, fell in the harbour running, caught his foot on the ropes. Then Mattie, just seven, went off with a promise, we never seen him come back, then Samuel … someone stole 'im away on one o' them Atlantic ships. And me, waiting for my ma who went into service: waitin', waitin'…

'But I sat it out, prayed like they told me, set out on the smacks, helpful as I can, never mind the cold got in my lungs. I remembered her saying, you wait Daniel, I'll come and get ye soon as I can.'

'Daniel? Your name's Daniel?'

The boy didn't acknowledge his question, carried on.

'So I'm waiting see, changes 'appen all the time don't they? They don't send kids out there no more, and I can still help where I can. Went back and forth to Dunkirk helping. They was that grateful, some of them, to see me. Some dying, praying they took their last breath on good ol' Blighty, not on no ferrin beach. Back and forth. And this lot here, all these nice boats with their fancy trimming, many a time I'm a-helping and they don't see me.'

'My name's Daniel too…'

'Oh aye? Well 'appen that was meant an all.'

As they were leaving Danny caught sight of the man standing by the window.

'Who's that?'

'Oh, he was after,' the boy said, 'one of them hundreds taken in from the sea.'

They parted by Jacob's Ladder.

'Show me the tunnels tomorrow?'

'We'll see,' the boy said. 'If I'm not needed anyplace else mebbe.'

Danny's phone rang as he was going up the High Street. It was Patrick. He thought of the room that was his alone.

'Yeah I'm fine. On me way … *home* … now, see you in a bit.' He smiled at the girl in the wheelchair outside the sweet shop. She smiled back.

The Year the Flamingos Came

The summer the flamingos came, Kerry rode the bus, the child inside her curled tight like a whelk. It was 1975. Pegwell Bay came into sight: the Hoverport. A chorus arose, women out of their seats, skin and cotton, nylon, tweed, shoulders.

'Bleeding heck!'

'What are they, storks or summat?'

'Herons, ain't they?'

'They're never herons! They's flaming flamingos they is! We saw them when we took our lot to Florida last year. Remember I brought in the photos?'

Cars had pulled in by the Viking Ship, and people were getting out. Their driver slowed down and Kerry pressed her nose against the glass. Flamingos they certainly were. A flock of some two-dozen neon ballerinas, incongruous on the mudflats. Beyond them the Channel hovered, still and grey. Beside them, a hovercraft waiting, and two figures digging bait.

Kerry felt her heart leap as she watched them. Home birds. They were home birds. Around her the women were still flaffing. The child inside her flipped as if in response, a light ripple.

'Do you think they got beached like that poor whale last year?'

'I dunno! Maybe they got blown in with the wind or something!'

'There weren't no wind last night! News said we're in for a long hot summer!'

Their faces steamed the glass. The flamingos became hazy and disappeared as the bus cruised out into the slow-moving traffic. They slipped out of Kerry's vision.

Around her, the factory flock settled down, apart from Beth, who took the opportunity to light up, settling her reed-thin hips against the back of her seat, continuing the tale of awe with her neighbour. The thin wisp of smoke curled away from her conductor's hand, mimicking the tail of a kite in a robust wind.

'Well, you never bleeding know, you never bleeding know, do ya? I tell you it's a sign that; mark my words.'

'They was bold as brass weren't they? Not that I know nuttin 'bout birds, but them lot wasn't them that come every year was they?'

'No, they ain't. Hey! You don't reckon they escaped from a zoo or something, do you? Or that circus? They was putting up posters at the Lord of the Manor...'

'Them kind o' birds don't do tricks you dumb twit!'

'Oo you calling dumb Irene? You didn't even know what they was called, you was calling them herons!'

Laughter bounced off the seats like party balloons, each ear catching its sound, magnifying it, carrying it forwards and backwards, soaring on a ripple of words.

Kerry looked across through the window on the land side. The towers of the power station loomed upwards, grey and austere but tucked in at the waist into matronly bell-like shapes. Behind them the country was flat and uninteresting, the squat buildings of the fireworks factory like a sketch, only broken by the barest glimpse of the ruined walls of Richborough Fort. Someone had told her it had been there since the Romans. The bus was approaching the factories, and the turgid smell from the polluted sea entered, replacing the air of jollity with its insidious presence. Beth ground her cigarette out into the ashtray on the arm of the seat, and the rustling of bags replaced the chatter, the spread of breezeblock and corrugated buildings coming into view, the bus slowing down, pulling into the concrete yard.

The bathing hat slipped beneath Kerry's fingers, the wheel slicing it neatly. She sighed. She was never going to get the hang of this. Around her, strips of decimated rubber decorated her workbench. The noise from the machines filled the workshop, hummed and rattled; women's fingers flew, heads bowed, words and brief bursts of laughter breaking through Radio 2 on the loudspeaker. The DJ, Terry Wogan, joked about it only being 200 shopping days to Christmas.

The smell of sulphur snaked in from the back, the men shifting trays of rubber into a cavern of heat. All day long banter cut and thrust between them and the women on the shop-floor. The taste of rubber clung to their tongues. The heat influenced the way they moved in their overalls, unbuttoned to the waist. Cigarettes hung from their lips by the open hangar door. Waves of cool air ushered in constant moans of complaint.

'Shut that bleeding door!'

'Bit o' fresh air, put hair on yer chest, you lot!'

'Whadda *you* know Frank? You ain't got neither!'

'More belly than chest, that one!'

'You should bleeding stay 'ome you lot, get yer husbands' tea on time!'

The girl next to her had mastered it already. A neat pile

of swimming hats lay in her tray. The supervisor had come round, and had looked down at Kerry's massacred strips with thin, pursed lips.

She got up to go to the loo, feeling the supervisor's eyes on her. Five minutes, she mouthed.

Two of the women from the bus were smoking over the sink. They glanced swiftly over at Kerry and carried on their conversation.

She went in and sat on the loo. She didn't even want a wee. She just wanted to sit for a minute out of the clatter and hum. She felt useless. Now she was pregnant she was going to be even more useless. She'd been on hot water bottles all through her trial period here. She didn't know why they moved her to swim-hats. Maybe the season had something to do with it.

Words winged their way over the toilet cubicle. 'They're taking on another bunch of new ones next week.'

'Chrissake, another six months and they'll be threatening redundancies again. Did you see the news last night about the pits? Blighters weren't happy with closin' down Chislet; first excuse was no more steam trains, now they're going on about steel. Happen there won't be no call fer it one day.'

'That'll never happen. That can't happen. You can't take away work like that from men. And they'll always need coal, folk'll always need coal.'

'Well the way they was talking it didn't sound too good. Don't know what my Jim would do if he ever lost his job.'

'Shouldn't worry about it love. Anyroad, we'd better go before that jumped-up chargehand has something to say.'

Back at her bench, Kerry picked up another two sections of semi-circular rubber. Beth glanced over at her. 'How you getting on, ducks?'

Kerry met her eyes sheepishly. 'I'm not really.' She

looked enviously over at Beth's bench. Scores of neatly beaded swim-hats sat waiting for collection. Curved like slices of watermelon, a rainbow stack of lemons and lilacs. Beth's hands sped round the wheel; perfect hats fell into her basket. Kerry had a moment of déjà vu, but it wouldn't reveal itself to her.

Beth's hands stilled for a moment then she beckoned her over. ' 'Ere. Come and watch me for a minute.' Kerry slid off her seat and walked round the bench. Beth held up the two offending pieces of rubber.

'First thing ducks, think; think of the money. Think how much extra in that little brown envelope on a Thursday for every thousand of these. Next, think: plonkers. Who'd wear shit like this? Not me, you wouldn't even get me in no chlorine pool. Ramsgate beach under a sunshade, that'll do. So think of them heads like Humpty Dumpty and stick 'em together. These two pieces here, they're sweethearts, see? They want to be together, sweet and close as a seam. Take your time, slide it, feed it with both fingers like if you're knitting, fingers working together then zip! There you are. If you're no good at this, they'll have you doing French letters, and you won't like that. Never hear the end of it!'

Kerry giggled, then put her hand to her mouth, as Beth was as serious as a Preacher on Good Friday. She didn't let on she knew nothing about knitting.

At lunchtime she went into the canteen for a cuppa, unfolding her sandwiches at one of the Formica tables. Sue from hot water bottles joined her.

'Hiya Kerry, how you doing in swimming hats?'

Sue was tiny, with a sleek head of black hair that swung above her shoulders.

Kerry sighed. 'Not very good. Dunno why they moved me. I was getting on fine in bottles.'

'Orders, I suppose. They do it all the time, you can't get

too comfy. You'll get the hang of it, don't worry.'

'They were talking redundancies in the loo...'

'They do that all the time! Gossipy old bags!'

Kerry laughed.

'You gotta remember ... oh but you won't know this not coming from round here ... them wimmin 'ere ain't long been earning good money. Most, like me mum, come off the land, picking spuds and cabbages and apples in all weathers. These here wages are bloody good money, 'specially if you can top it up with extra. Some even take plugs 'ome to assemble, sit in front the telly, click click bloody click. But the bloody men are still holding out their bleeding hands come Thursday payday! Tell you what, though, I ain't sticking round here long if I can help it, I'm gonna get a nice clean job working in Chelsea Girl or somewhere like that.'

They downed tools sharp at 4.45. Ten minutes to tidy up, do time sheets, visit the loo. At 4.55 they put coats on, made their way to the double doors. At 5 the siren went, trilling through the factory. Doors swung open all along the concrete walkway, women emerging from workshop doors gabbling and joining the throng, heading to the buses. Kerry thought of it as the Avenue of the Farmyard, it reminded her of her grandmother's geese, her father's cows.

The Saturday past, one of the girls had got married. On the Friday, her workmates dressed her up in strips of rubber for a wedding gown, complete with train, weighed her down with Durex condoms ringed with plastic flowers, adorning her head like a veil, and made her walk down the yard, laughter and well wishers all breaking out of the workshop doors. The comments were ribald and coarse, and Kerry had felt shame for the girl. There was no way she would ever sacrifice herself so.

She'd forgotten about the flamingos. As the bus slowed

down through Cliffsend, she noticed the cars lining the side of the road, the crowds and the cameras. Hand-held cameras took their place alongside those on tripods. They were filming the flamingos, pinning their elegance down on the mudflats.

She turned the key to her flat, her fingers sore from practising on the wheel all day. A letter lay on the door mat. The familiar stamp brought a smile to her face. But the worry lurched inside her, reminding her. She read it at the dining table, drinking tea. The first part of her mother's letters were always full of warnings. She mustn't wear her skirts too short or forget where she came from. She must eat enough greens. She must be careful not to make friends with people before she knew them. Most of all she must stay away from those English boys, they thought foreign girls were easy pickings. Had she found a congregation yet? She thanked her for the small money order she'd sent, hoped she was getting to grips with her job at the bank. Everybody at home was so proud of her. They were hoping her sister Evangeline would be able to join her soon.

She folded the letter back into the envelope and sat looking out onto the communal courtyard. The people in the flat above had left their rubbish at the side of the bin again. But she couldn't complain, look what she had had to do to get this place.

The flamingos were on the Southern News. An expert said it was highly unusual that flamingos would migrate this far. Most likely they were blown off course, or perhaps the predicted warm weather blew them here. No one knew how long they would stay. Perhaps they were just resting.

Before she went to sleep, Kerry remembered what Beth's hands, spinning over the wheel, reminded her of. It was a storybook image: Rumpeltstiltskin, spinning straw into gold, and the princess standing before him afraid, commanded to do the same.

Her sister Evangeline's face swum before her as she fell asleep. When she dreamed, Rumpeltstiltskin came into the room. He wore the face of her landlord.

Alice

They hadn't been out long when they realised they stood out like fairies in a farmyard: hair bouncy and flicked like Farrah Fawcett's; maxi dresses. They'd gone over to Broadstairs on the bus, light-headed and giggling after two glasses of Martini. They'd had a smoke already – Neil had rolled two when they were there, which they'd shared over the heads of the kids in the living room. He was full of himself as being the good dad, 'letting' Laurie out whilst he minded the kids. But Spurs were on, and two beers and an eighth of Moroccan were all it took to keep him happy.

On the top deck of the bus Laurie lit a John Players, and moaned about Neil all the way along the Ramsgate Road, what a skank he was and how all week she couldn't wait for Friday. Alice nodded, she too; what a week, what a boring week, up in the mornings, kids to school, hoovering, nursery, tea.

They talked about how long it had been since they'd

been out, before Christmas, with the guys, sitting in the Royal at Ramsgate chasing tequilas. Sandy had got them into that lark, fresh back from Spain and showing off. Neil and Sam had lapped it all up, making plans for them all to go over in the summer, then slagging Sandy off later, what a wanker he was.

They got off the bus in Queen's Road and headed down Broadstairs High Street. No-one else was wearing long dresses. Below them the sea glittered. It was late spring and getting lighter in the evenings. They poked their heads round the door of The Albert, and just as quickly pulled back. There were only old people in there, guarding their pints. At the corner of Albion St the wind caught them, whipping their maxi skirts around their ankles.

'I'm flipping freezing, wish I'd worn my coat!'
'Yeah, me and all! Where shall we go?'
'The Rose?'
'Dickens?'
'Dunno, s'a bit early, don't get going till around nine.'
'Yeah but I couldn't wait to get out the house!'
'Me too!'
'How about one in the Tartar Frigate to start off?'
'You're on.'

They headed down to the harbour, through the York Gate. A blast of sea air blew them in. Couples were sitting at the tables, a bunch of guys at the bar turned round as they entered. That was the main problem with the place, you couldn't enter discreetly. They headed for the Ladies, taking turns to use the mirror, brushing their hair back into place. At the bar, Alice stood back and let Laurie take charge.

'Right, what you having?'

The guys, business-looking types, moved aside with open smiles on their faces. One said 'All right, ladies?' Laurie ordered a shandy and a Martini, and they made their way to the table in the window. It was a good clocking spot, just by the door. The wind blew in young girls, laughing. College types, expensive tapered straights and Levi jackets. Alice shifted in her seat.

'Did you think any more about that job?' Laurie shook her out of thinking about the Vogue magazines she used to buy. She shrugged. Factory work was all she was good for.

'Why not try the Hypermarket? Be quite nice waltzing round there, beats fitting plugs.'

'Yeah I could, I suppose. '

'Me mum used to work up that way, at Haine Hospital, and Jill … my sister Jill, she … they admitted her there after the first time, you know…'

'Oh yeah, I'm sorry, they moved Jill didn't they…?'

Laurie nodded and looked out at the window, at the white timbers of The Old Lookout on the pier, fading in the dying light.

'Yes, she's at Chartham now.'

'Oh.'

A burst of laughter broke from the men at the bar as a head, wearing a green Mohican, poked round the door and just as quick withdrew.

'Did you see that? The punks are in!' The guy wise-cracking looked in their direction and winked.

Alice and Laurie giggled.

'Shall we have another one here or do you want to go somewhere else?'

It was ten deep at the bar in the Dickens. A carnival of faces and bodies dressed in glitter and heat. Laurie pushed Alice forward, telling her she was skinnier. She ducked under the armpits of guys raising jugs of beer to their lips. There were strong wisps of Brut aftershave. Some let her through, one or two called her 'Babe'. Another, an older guy, said 'Young Lady'.

She felt lightheaded already. Laurie had given her a slice of cannabis cake before they came out. She'd been a bit hesitant but Laurie had insisted. 'Go on, it'll relax you.'

Well it was doing something, she felt very giggly. The man who called her 'Young Lady' suddenly looked like a walrus. She was just about to say something when she realised she was at the bar. The guy serving was giving change the same time as asking her what she would like. She might have been cold outside, but here, leaning on the bar, her bare arms were alive. She didn't know why, they just tingled with nakedness, even the impression of her elbows on the wood sent messages up her arms.

She was getting her money out when a voice behind her said, 'Here, I'll get this.' A fiver flashed like a bird's wing. It was Walrus Head. She protested, he waved a hand saying, 'Fine, Fine.' She grimaced to herself but gave up the fight.

She mumbled her gratitude, squeezed her way back through the crowd to Laurie, standing by the DJ. She leaned over and tried to communicate the news about the free drink but the music was throbbing, so gave up.

In the interval she spotted Walrus Head looking over in her direction. She quickly adjusted her gaze, coming to rest on a guy in a denim jacket. He was a pony, grey, dappled. She liked ponies. She smiled. She thought about sex with Sam suddenly, knowing he'd be waiting up for her. He liked to see her 'done up' as he called it, liked the thought that guys looked at her like that but she was his only. He liked the smell of cigarettes and drink on her too; weird.

They ended up staying in the Dickens until eleven, then got the last bus back to Ramsgate, getting off at the harbour. They started the walk along the promenade to Nero's Nightclub. They'd considered going to The Moonlighters at Pegwell, but too many of their friends went there. Alice remembered grinding to James Brown there with Alfie, whose long blond hair she'd always found a turn on, but she'd married Sam so that was that. She was ashamed to remember snogging Alfie though, at the back of the fire escape. God, what a slut. Just as well he moved away.

The boats were singing against their moorings in the marina, the moonlight dancing on the water. Alice could hear the fish in the chorus. Cod, she reckoned. Cod harmonies. They fished for cod, didn't they? Or was it herrings? Laurie pointed out the fancy yacht that belonged to that actor from the *General Hospital* TV series. It had been in the paper. They walked past the old Customs House, the odd spill of music still coming out from a lock-in at The Queens Head. A drunk sat on the concrete boulders singing and eating fish and chips. The fishing boats slumbered silent by the pier. She remembered hearing something about the industry dying. About cod wars. She hoped not. She and Sam liked to watch the boats come in, the gulls escorting them like pissed bridesmaids. The lights were out by Harrison's Restaurant. Pleasurama too. A pong of seaweed came from the outgoing tide.

'Here, have one of these,' Laurie pressed a tablet into her palm.

'No, Laurie, not pills, no.'

'C'mon don't be a spoilsport! It's only speed!'

'No.'

'You really need to lighten up Alice…'

'Lors I've had lager, three Martinis, a blow and a slice of your cake! What do you think I am, a flaming druggie?'

Laurie laughed, and lit up a joint. 'Okay, Miss Prude, have a blow then. Here, Neil did us one.'

Alice looked around; there was a small group behind them, a couple of guys ahead. She slowed and waited for the group to pass. They clip-clopped past like ponies.

A few cars passed them; one slowed and a fat guy hung his ass through a back window.

'Fucking creep,' Laurie shouted. The pungent aroma of hash anointed the air.

She passed the joint to Alice.

'Hope nobody smells this,' Alice said nervously.

'Sure beats shit outa the smell of seaweed,' Laurie laughed, then bent over, doubled-up with laughter.

'Sure beats shit … sure beats shit…!' Her laughter rose up into the night air, and Alice's joined hers. She wasn't cold any more, and felt strong enough to face the sharp guys with their New Romantic clothes and the girls with their trendy disco gear. Damn them. Maxi dresses weren't going out, they were coming back in.

The lights from the Bingo Hall went out as they passed, and giggles came from the helter-skelter and the waltzer.

'Sounds like someone's getting their skirt lifted!' Laurie laughed.

'Would you ever…?' Alice put the question.

'Screw someone else? Ah that would be telling wouldn't it?' She took the joint from her and laughed at Alice's face under the streetlamp. 'Lordy you are one gullible chick!'

'No I'm not!' Alice was suddenly afraid. Her feet appeared to be floating by themselves over the pavement.

'What's this stuff we're smoking?'

'Black. Moroccan. Good innit? Neil got an ounce from the Donoghues.'

'Umm.' She felt her arms grow light. 'I don't think I should have any more.'

'You'll be fine, get a couple of drinks down you.'

The queue for Nero's went round the block. Cars were double-parked across the road by the boarded-up swimming pool.

'Shame about that, innit? Me and Sam met there.'

'What, the pool?'

'Yeah, it was great on a sunny day. Don't know why they had to close it.'

She felt her feet then, cold toes through her sandals. Sam. Why was she here, when Sam was at home minding the kids? *Don't be pathetic. Who minds them all week, and on snooker nights?* She shook her head, trying to free her thoughts.

Around them groups of girls, dolled up to the nines in fashions Alice hadn't seen in Chelsea Girl or Dorothy Perkins, smoothed their sleek hair in the mirrors of small compacts. Their conversation was all guys and work. Alice didn't know what she would find to say to girls like that. Bet they didn't work evenings in a lousy factory.

The baby walked today, took two steps. He came up behind me suddenly in the kitchen like a freaky walking doll. Gave me a fright. Christ, how can you say that about your own baby?

'Here we go!' They watched as the two guys ahead of them got turned away for wearing jeans and trainers, then smiled as they got given the thumbs-up.

Music thrummed, underground rhythms snaking their way up the spiral staircase. The cloakroom girls stood waiting for coats. They stood very still behind the counter, Alice guessed their bottom bodies were lobsters, you could tell by the sharp way their red fingernails clutched at the tickets. She and Laurie hadn't come out with coats so moved on down to the Ladies, full with flocks of starlings and parakeets, fingers fluffing hair, unrolling tubes of crimson lipstick. *What is 'in'?* Alice tried not to stare at herself in the mirror. She stood behind the younger girls as if giving way. *I have a man. I have a man at home.*

Laurie sprayed some perfume on her without asking and poked her in the back.

'Come on,' she said. 'You're wasting good drinking time, dancing time, and pinching bums time!'

She floated down the spiral staircase. Her head beginning to feel large, very large. She tried to shake the feeling away, her hand gripping the rail as she descended. A young guy in a blue Hawaiian shirt was blocking her way. He was coming up. He stood and waited for her to move, smiling.

'You don't half look like Stevie Nicks,' he said.

Her fingers let go of the rail and she wobbled. His arms stretched out in a flash and caught her.

'Oops!' he said, winking at Laurie. 'Looks like someone's had a few!'

'She's fine, let her go,' Laurie snapped. She linked arms with Alice and marched her down the stairs.

They entered a wall of sound and blood red decor, Roman columns, reclining sedans, plush carpet, mosaics that looked as if they had been lifted from Vesuvius. Psychedelic patterns splattered the dance-floor from a revolving glitter-ball. Duran Duran wailed around the walls.

'God, I love this place!' Laurie hugged her, then dragged her to the bar. She looked in her purse after she paid, and screwed her face up. 'They really rip you off in here! Twice the price of the pub! Oh well we'll have to get some poor sucker to buy us a drink. Come on.'

'Where are we going?' Alice was reluctant to move. She was happy to stop right here and stare. Stare at all the beautiful people in their trendy clothes, all the new disco gear, their spandex miniskirts; listen to their breaking laughter, watch the watchers circling the dance floor, bare but for a few, hungry to move before it was cool to. They were amazing to watch, even those who were hardly moving. The light dipped and fell on their bodies making them look like fluorescent fish. One girl was spinning round and round, her elbows like fins. It was like looking in an aquarium, like the one at Palm Bay. Well maybe not Palm Bay, Brighton. She wanted to join them, those discordant girls. That's where she wanted to be, to let her hair down, fling her head back, free her body from the sameness of everyday. She wanted to spin and spin like a whirling dervish, to have the unexpected possess her.

But Laurie was tugging at her arm: 'C'mon.'

They were going 'for a walk' she said. Alice limped behind her, her foot hurting. She must have twisted it on the staircase. Or maybe the long walk up from the harbour. They squeezed through groups and couples, some with heads back laughing, or with eyes roaming. Some dropped and fixed on her and Laurie, some swiftly looked past them, their eyes like torches.

Some of the girls wore gold lamé and Lycra, exposing bra straps and bellies, slinky in tight-fitting jumpsuits, like Hot Gossip off the telly. She should have known that Ramsgate wasn't that far behind when it came to fashion, why didn't she pay attention? She should have walked round Etam yesterday. Her maxi dress skirted her ankles, as if to taunt her. She wished she could rip it off, be left standing there in something tight-fitting and sparkly. Her face began to go hot and cold.

The 'walk' included intermittent pauses around the dance floor. Strange creatures posed by the columns, some in hats and bright clothes, with elongated ears and mirrored eyes. Their eyes spotlit each other, those approaching, those on the dance-floor. Their limbs alternated between beats, in the beat, became the beat. Movement, light, hot bodies. Laurie was shouting into the ear of some guy, then disappeared. Alice forced herself back to lean against a pillar. The room had begun to shrink right before her eyes, the creatures around her becoming rodents and turtles, all scrambling around her ankles and circling her voluminous skirt which floated out into the room like a tent. She squeezed her eyes shut.

'Hey, Stevie, how you doin?'

An arm snaked around her shoulder. From the slit that were her eyes flowers danced.

'You fancy a dance?' Hawaiian Shirt.

Laurie swung round from the bar with a huge smile on her face. She plunged a glass into Alice's hand. 'Here, grab this. Complimentary.'

'Complimentary?' Alice looked vague. Laurie smiled and nodded at the guy standing next to her. It was Walrus

Head.

Alice suddenly felt sick. She wandered off and found herself on the dance floor. Hibiscus flowers were floating in front of her eyes. Bodies were morphing into odd shapes, hemming her in. She pushed her arms out into the heady surf. Lips brushed her cheek. Words tried to reach her ear. She allowed herself to be led.

She sat on one of the red chaises longues. Hawaiian Shirt disappeared and came back with a Coke.

'Here, drink this, you look hot.'

She held the glass against her face. Cool. She caught her breath.

'You okay?'

She nodded.

'You want to get some fresh air?'

'No. No. Thank you, but I'm married.'

'Married girls can breathe too!'

Despite herself, she laughed. She looked closely at him. He was actually quite cute, dark curly hair and blue eyes. He peered closely at her.

'You're stoned,' he said, smiling. 'Not good for you, really.'

Was he for real?

'Oh well, what's good for us really? Maggie Thatcher? The Falklands War? Alar on apples?'

'Woah!'

'Alice!' Laurie appeared at her side. 'Alice, come and have a dance!'

'No I'm having a break, you carry on.'

'OOO! Hark at you!' She pulled a face, and in the flickering light her face looked grotesque and bright red, her hair like antlers. She crossed her arms and looked down at Alice crossly. Then turned and stamped off.

'She's a bit of a drama queen!' Hawaiian Shirt said.

Alice shrugged. 'She'll get over it.'

Her eyes were drawn to the dance floor. An old woman

had joined the dancers but stood there, watching, dressed in wellies and a grey raincoat. She had very long, thin grey hair.

As Alice watched, the woman began to copy the moves she was seeing, following one dancer and then another, wide arms circling like a helicopter. She might have been practising Tai Chi. She began to move faster, her hair spinning like a plastic windmill fringed with feathers. The glitterball poured down fragments of coloured rain. Her hips jerked spasmodically, laden by the stomping rise and fall of her wellies. The other dancers began to notice her, and moved aside, not wanting her to pollute their youth and energy, interrupt the flow of their sinuous and sexually-charged movements. Those near to Alice were laughing, raising their glasses like goblets, banging on the sides of them with cigarette lighters and car keys. They began to chant 'Go, Go, Go !' and their chants soon raised above the music, adding another level to the drum bass vibrating from the floor, up and along the Roman columns and shivering the overhead revolving disco balls to spin faster and faster, spraying their hallucinogenic lights like the Snow Queen's splintered shards of glass.

Alice knew it was time to leave. She rose with a sudden gravitational pull that helped to propel her through the throng, changing shape as she squeezed under arms, breaking through interlocked couples, the bow-and-arrow curves of satin-clad backs, the laces of culottes, the eyes of diamantes. Her feet became a fawn's, small-hoofed and dainty as they negotiated the mosaic floor, her elbows morphing from bone to feather, giving her flight up the spiralled stairs and out into the foyer where the bouncers turned and opened the door where the wind was waiting. Waiting to guide her along the dark streets, over the tops of houses, the invisible presence of the silent sea, the boats chorusing in their moorings. The moon offered a slice of her light, just enough to grant Alice vision, not enough to make her prey for those sad and lonely men who had waited so long on the sides of dance floors to pluck up the courage to ask girls to dance, and who now prowled the streets in rusting Ford Escorts for girls like her. Her maxi skirt became a sail, buffeting her along the seafront and along the London Road into the solid arms of her house, her waiting husband, her sleeping child. She turned the key and floated upwards, blinking free of the dark.

The Airman

For Steven

Four-thirty in the morning was the best time. He liked nothing better than to wander out of the Portakabin and watch the sun rise out of the sea like a carnival spider appearing above a wall. Its ascension set the horizon ablaze, a wild frenzy of oil and water running into a blood-red, kerosene sky. He would feel himself climbing with it; tying into his recurrent dreams that, for some reason, he had yet to decipher.

The moment would not last. Soon the vividness would run into pastel and the whitewash of a new day would spread across the sky, the solid shapes of the ferry and cargo boats steal the vista on the water. The guys who had worked the night shift with him would stumble out from behind cramped computer desks, pour unfinished mugs of coffee down the sink, gather up the empty cans of lager and porn videos, and make their way out to their parked cars.

Nick was never in a hurry. He had no wife or children to rush home for. He could dally as long as he liked, file the export sheets tidily for the day shift, and banter with them between half-smoked stubs of Marlboroughs. He was always ready with a crack and a quip, laughter on the edge of every exchange. He could linger long enough to order breakfast from the café, dark and full of the unwashed bodies of Continental drivers and dark black cigarettes, before heading to the flat in Artillery Road. Sometimes he would get waylaid, dropping into the Foy Boat pub for a coffee and a Scotch, a temporary rejuvenation before the fall into the abyss of sleep, often with his shoes still on.

He had no trouble sleeping. Not for him the complaints like Clint, bleary eyed at the start of a night shift, staring down at the manifest as he moaned about the baby crying and his wife's clumsy footsteps round the house. Time and again he said he'd be looking for another job.

Nick could sleep through a hurricane. Neither the passing traffic nor the constant pings of the newsagents' door downstairs kept him awake. The dreams kept him pinned to the pillow as if by force. He woke promptly at five, showered and headed for the Foy Boat.

In the eight years he'd been here, he'd slipped into a comfortable routine. He liked the hustle and bustle of the port, liked to watch the ferries and the cargo boats and yachts slide in and out of the harbour. In between, he filed manifests, listed cargo, and filled in Customs and Excise sheets.

The threat of change always loomed, with a history of roll-on roll-off owners – Olsen, Townsend, the Sally Line. He watched passengers set off on the booze cruise, saw them return with car boots full of wine and cigarettes. At the edge of his knowledge flickered Romans and Vikings, the French, King Henry. Closer to home were the disappearing fishing vessels that once offered fresh herring on the harbour, and the sleek, expensive yachts. What he did know, was that the Channel toyed with them all like a cat: they rode her, they sung on her, they dreamed on her, they ploughed galleons and drove slave ships through her, sent small boys out on her, submerged submarines and bargained with her in inclement weather; at her whim she offered them passage, set them on their way, teased them, tossed them, and many times drowned them. Painters came and painted her, sung to her, praised the light, the breeze and the waters, engineers burrowed through her belly, and pledged to plant tall masts in her to plunder the wind.

Nick pushed sheets of paper across a Formica desk, shared the hours of darkness with other men who depended on the sea for a living. He walked daily down to the sea, with a lit cigarette and a step that echoed down through the tarmac to a strata of mud and bone, chalk and shell.

He would think briefly of the tunnels running beneath him, dug into the chalk, hiding places, smugglers' hoards and wartime refuge; dens now for teenage boys who forced their way through padlocked entrances and boarded up exits to practise their right to be explorers and rebels. He couldn't blame them, reacting against a childhood dulled by TV screens. His own childhood, running wild on the Norfolk coast, had been uncensored. Off on his bike from dawn till dusk, with fishing rod and box for gathering wild birds' eggs. No 'Mind how you cross the road'. His parents hailed from another time. They were now both dead, not long after they had exchanged Hunstanton for Ramsgate, exchanging their old cottage for a nuclear, soulless council flat surrounded by strangers on the Newington Estate. His mother had been haunted by a Ramsgate childhood, the imagined memory of the sea.

He held sunrise in his mind, imagining the other half of the world where the sun had just left, night falling there, on cold lands, on tropic lands, on seas too wide to imagine. And he wondered why he dreamt of skies instead of seas. For in those dreams he was flying a Spitfire, wearing goggles and a jacket made of leather, and he turned to his navigator and said, 'Just one more drop and we're home free.' It wasn't clear if he was keeping the German guns surrounding Dunkirk at bay, returning from a mission, or if he was a First World War pioneer. It was certainly a Spitfire, not a bi-plane, but time didn't seem to be fixed in the cockpit. He suspected his navigator didn't even come from the same time as he did. The land beneath scalloped the sea, and the waves were crests of grass undulating to an immortal jet stream. As he pressed the lever for the bombs to drop, the only thing that dropped was the Spitfire, falling from the sky to a bonanza of fireballs and blackness.

He couldn't tell this to the girl he had met at the weekend. She was small, like a doll, she only came up to his shoulders. She had a head of dark gold and a moody smile. He had turned from the bar to look down at her small hands clutching a fiver, waiting to be served. He moved aside, a pint clasped tightly in his hand, a cigarette in the other. He heard her order white wine and watched her move to a table where she kept her eye on the door. He didn't know why he kept looking at her, pretty as she was. He wasn't short of women; he had been enjoying the attentions of a married woman whose husband conveniently worked in Saudi Arabia. The guys all teased his lucky escape so far from female entanglement. The door opened several times, but no one joined her. She came up to the bar again and asked to use the phone. He turned to her then and asked if he could buy her a drink, but she refused.

That would have been it, his apologetic smile, a shrug of his shoulders.

And then, on Sunday morning after the nightshift, their paths crossed on Jacob's ladder, those steps carved into the cliffs. He looked up, and there she was descending. He waited in the shadow of the Sailor's Church, turning up his collar, conscious of the taste of stale beer and cigarettes about him.

'Hi there!'

She paused, the light of recognition coming slowly into her eyes. 'Oh, hello.'

'You're up and about early.'

'I was hoping to catch the sunrise,' she adjusted the camera strap on her shoulder. 'But I think I've missed it.'

He cast his eyes up knowledgeably. 'Yes, by an hour or so.'

'Damn. Oh well – maybe I can get some early morning shots.'

He lingered. 'Is this work, or a hobby?'

'Both,' she laughed.

'Why don't you tell me about it over a coffee?'

He noticed the brief suspicion in her eyes, but then she straightened her shoulders and said, 'Why not?'

The café under the cliff offered pungent morning smells of coffee and bacon. It was a haunt of lorry drivers and yachtsmen. Her bronze curls and sea-green eyes settled incongruously against the dark walls and cracked leather jackets. His tiredness disappeared, the words between them moving easily as they talked light and shade, sunrise, mornings, and the port. Later, he could have kicked himself as he tumbled into bed. They had not exchanged names.

But then something happened that took his mind away, as it did the minds of many others. He woke up to news that the passenger walkway between the ferry and the quayside had collapsed suddenly, killing six passengers and injuring several more. The port was in an uproar. The BBC cameras were leaf-cutter ants wielding the antennae of their equipment. Way into the future the questions and answers and seeking of blame would become a long drawn-out affair that would never be completely resolved. Full compensation would never be paid – the fight would be strung out in European courts for years against the Scandinavian owners. The Vikings had struck again.

He was distracted by a call from his lover, and he found himself walking up to the quiet cul-de-sac in Broadstairs on a Thursday daytime. She opened the door with a Martini in hand, wearing nothing more than a shortie nightgown.

He'd been here before, of course, settled into the leather sofa, refusing to focus on the photographs on the mantelpiece, Ava and the husband smiling into the camera, the school photographs, a girl conveniently away at a private school in Canterbury. They always had sex in the spare bedroom, an anonymous room, which apart from the double bed and an oak chest only bore one point of focus – a Turner reproduction of a Margate sunset over a vivid sea. The colours would always explode before his eyes as he came, she above him like the figurehead of a sailing ship, her breasts dewy with sweat and her head falling back, leaving her throat, a marble column above his hungry mouth.

But this time, the painting above Ava's back appeared to be drawing him into its very substance. The abstractions of light began to blind him, and the sea opened, sucking him into its watery depths. He caught his breath, and as he breathed out his body grew cold.

'What's the matter, Hun?' She stopped moving, and her brown eyes swum above him.

He managed a smile. 'Hey, it's nothing, I'll be OK in a bit.' But he wasn't.

She brought them up coffees and told him not to worry. They talked about the walkway and the deaths, the mangled wreckage, the newsmen like ants wandering in and out of the Portakabin.

'It's bound to affect you,' she said, 'plus all those night shifts! It's not natural, is it? Maybe you should do something else.'

Her words followed him as he left, deciding to walk back along the beach to Ramsgate. The tide was in, so he cut through King George VI Park, where a crowd of parakeets jeered him, anointing the sky with flashes of fluorescent green. The sea shadowed his passage across the green, flickering between the wild plants and saplings taking over the railings. He imagined a time when they would completely obliterate the view of the sea. At the exit gate, the Channel possessed the horizon again, escorting him as he hit concrete, stepping past the ambitious amphitheatre some benefactor had bestowed on the town, aware of the tunnels beneath his feet again, ghostly train tracks, smugglers' vertebrae rich with calcium deposits, fossils and DNA. He walked the promenade past the Granville Theatre where the posters hinted at more ghostly gatherings, clamouring for his attention – ribald seaside singalongs, amateur dramatic versions of Gilbert and Sullivan, second-rate comedians, thigh-slapping panto Jacks. Then down towards the harbour with its carnivalesque collection of boats.

Since the accident he had been unable to welcome the sunrise on the quayside. He found it slightly distasteful to stand within the shadows where people had died. No matter how philosophical he had tried to be, it had ceased to be something in which he could find not only pleasure, but a connection to.

He remembered Clint mentioning there was a job going at Manston Airport, freight forwarding. Maybe it was time to make a move. Not that he knew anything about planes, or precisely what they did there, victim of the ranting of the press as they all were, failed plans for passenger flights and complaints about night flights from those foolish enough to live in the flight path. But he imagined the sunrise over the open fields was just as spectacular.

He bought himself a paper, scanning the Job Vacancies briefly before turning into the Foy Boat for a pint. The girl with the moody eyes was sitting in the bay window. He paused.

'Waiting for someone?'

'Perhaps,' she said.

The Three Sisters

Thanatos stood outside his restaurant, a fat cigar between his fingers. The traffic rolled past unceasingly along Northdown Road. His mind wandered to a time when tractors chugged along this road, trailers packed high with cabbages. Thanet's all bloody cabbages, they used to say. They'd have come through from St Peter's where now the fields that were left were only just holding on to the grass verges against the onslaught of housing estates, the sea across Palm Bay laughing with its continuous presence.

Next door the blokes were hauling in a large sofa off the pavement, making room for matching chairs and a table that had seen better days. Thanatos and his wife had discussed putting chairs and tables outside, to give it a more continental air, like Brighton. Time was you couldn't even get away with a sandwich board, the council'd come down on you like a ton of bricks. Now everyone, it seemed, was doing it. Some pavements you took your life in your hands stepping out in the road, weaving in and out of tables full of plants, rabbit hutches and sale rails from the charity shops. Some said the road was going downhill. Thanatos didn't agree with that, he liked change and challenge. He thought about the hotels running down to the sea, once full of tourists, now becoming bedsits and homes for refugees.

Behind him the aroma of cumin and garlic curled through the door. His wife's voice curled with it, chiding the young lad they'd just taken on. Thanatos drew on his cigar, Cuban of course, hand-rolled in that factory outside Havana where instead of Radio 2's Ken Bruce a Caribbean lilt read stories over the tannoy. If it weren't for the time his wife had spent shitting his money out, he would have called it the holiday of a lifetime. In and out them special tourist gift shops when he'd have been happy to sit on the pavement and be entertained by the wandering musicians, and look at the girls. He dispelled the image of his wife stirring the couscous and turned his thoughts instead to the most beautiful woman he had ever seen rolling this very cigar through her swift and dancing fingers, fleet and light as a mosquito, her smoky eyes and wide mouth reaching down into his trousers already damp from the heat. What a night he could have had with such a woman! He closed his eyes and rolled his lips over the cigar.

'Tani!' His wife's sharp voice cut into his thoughts. 'Tani I thought you were going to Bookers? We're out of bleeding tomatoes and it's eleven o'clock already! Wassamadder with you? Staring into space as if I haven't got enough trouble with that stupid boy you brought in!'

'Give it a rest, willya? I'm just having a quick smoke before I go up there. You don't want me smoking in the car, do ya?'

'Well it don't look good you smoking in front the business does it? Who's gonna want to eat in a place where a fat ugly man in a holey jumper blowing smoke in the blinking doorway?'

Thanatos groaned and stubbed the end of his cigar out between his thumbnails, flicking the embers, which fell like stars and died on the pavement. He wondered briefly if the Cuban girl smoked; he'd seen women smoking cheroots, but they were mannish women, lesbian types who didn't know how to dress. He looked at his wife standing in the doorway, her breasts heaving under the bodice of her overall. She didn't look that bad for her age really, eyes still clear and grey, good skin that some English women had the grace and genes to keep. He wondered fleetingly how differently things would have turned out if he'd married a Greek woman.

He leaned towards her and rubbed a smoky thumb along her cheek. 'Right dahling, hold yer horses, I'm off.'

He hadn't been long in the car when his phone went. He was waiting by the Cecil Square traffic lights and answered it without thinking.

'Daddy? Daddy?' Adrianna's voice crackled through the mobile. 'Daddy can you come and get me from work, I don't feel well.'

'What? What...'

The lights changed and he dropped the phone on his lap, jerking into gear. Why did women always have to choose the wrong time? He pulled away down the Margate Road and picked the phone up again.

'Whassamattawiv you? You was all right this morning!'

'No I wasn't, I told mum I didn't feel well. You driving? I know you're driving Daddy! Why you answering the phone and driving? Well, I'm waiting by Nandos.'

'Adrianna … Adrianna!' He shook the phone. She'd gone. Cut him off. Bloody hell. Bloody blinking effing hell. Wassamader wiv these women? *She'd* called *him* for Chrissake! Then she's telling him off. Never mind 'Daddy is it okay, Daddy can you, Daddy where are you?' The little … now he was gonna feel guilty because she was standing outside Nando's, poorly, or thinking she's poorly, and he was meant to grab a case of tomatoes from Bookers for the moussaka and be back in the restaurant by 12. Somebody was having a laugh; they were all bleeding having a laugh. He'd have to call Mandy, tell her. He reached for his phone, and then dropped it as he clocked the police car settled in opposite B&Q. Bloody bollocks, was this day going to get any worse?

His temper was close to boiling point by the time he reached the Westwood Cross roundabout. He cursed everyone he knew that had anything to do with anything: the council, the government, the town planners, supermarket chains and local builders. All to do with bloody money, effing traffic from nose to tail, and it was only a Wednesday. He'd heard all the arguments before the new shopping complex had even been built, and at first was all for it, why not? High Streets were dead, every plonker knew that. If they wanted to put it all in one place, bully for them. If he'd had the money he'd have bid for one of the units himself. Would have been the opportunity to raise the business up a bit, go upmarket as they say. The girls and Mandy would have all liked that for sure. He could still imagine it now, a new name, not necessarily Greek but something elegant like The Eaterie, with black and white decor, plush seating and the cooking area visible, pleasant staff, well-spoken girls wearing … his ideas ran out then, and he caught sight of his daughter standing outside Nando's wearing her cream and black jacket.

He pulled up and she slid in, her face small under her head of smooth black hair, a black polka dot bow on one side.

'You were ages,' she scowled. 'I could die.'

'What's the matter wiv you then? You look fine to me.'

'I feel sick, I told Mum this morning I did but she told me to shut up and get dressed. She was just going on about how I mucked up the last job and I'd better keep this one.

Honestly that's all she cares about.'

'Na, that ain't true, Babe, you know that. But things are tough, you know, bills to pay and all that.'

'So I'm expected to do shit am I?'

'Adrianna! Watch yer bleeding lip!'

'Sorry,' she mumbled.

He shook his head, pulling away from the Margate Road and headed towards Bookers. Do everything you can fer them and that's the thanks. His dad would sent him flying, he would. But you can't touch 'em now, can yer?

'Where we going? I want to go home, Dad!'

'I've gotta get tomatoes for your mum.'

'Oh Gawd! Can't you just get them from Sainsbury's?'

'Sainsbury's? You having a laugh aint you? You have any idea how much that'll cost?'

He saw her shrug from the corner of his eye. He sighed. Always trouble this one, in and out of jobs since she left school two years ago. Not interested in college. They'd tried her out in the restaurant at first but that had been a nightmare. Sullen; rude to the customers. Called the place a dive. Mandy had pulled her out before she could do any more harm. Customers were hard enough to come by with the sandwich bars, and pubs doing food all round their area. Tani remembered a time when Northdown Road was buzzing with traders. Starting from the posh end at Palm Bay, the long road down to Margate was heaving. He was a boy then, fresh from London, with his dad and his big ideas about making it. 'Yer got yer Indian and yer Chinee,' he'd said, 'time for this Greek. They'll be coming back from Kalimera gasping for retsinas and moussaka, you'll see.'

Fair enough, through the '70s they was thrivin'. Clientele from Variety at the Winter Gardens and the Theatre Royal – Jim Whatsisname, Norman Wisdom, the Two Ronnies … right through to punters from Butlins fancying a taste of real food, to what passed for local councillors entertaining big shots. His dad had big black and white photos of them entertainers, all signed, lining the walls. All in the cellar now, fading away in boxes. Mandy had wondered about taking them to the Antiques Roadshow, but he couldn't be stuffed. Ten a penny they were, these celebs.

Beside him his daughter sighed.

'We're nearly there now,' he coaxed, 'I won't be a minute.'

He pulled into the Bookers car park and nodded at his phone as he climbed out.

'Phone your mum, will you? She'll be tearing her hair out.'

It was half twelve before he got back with the tomatoes. As expected, Mandy had a face like aubergines, grabbing the box from him as he came in the back door. She shouted at the boy to hurry up with the dishes. She didn't spot Adrianna at first, and only did that as her daughter attempted to disappear upstairs.

'What the…! Hey up, you! What the blinking hell are you doing home?' She spun round to Thanatos. 'Did she come in with you?'

'She rung me, said she didn't feel well. Had to pick her up at Westwood.'

'Didn't feel well? Not that one again! Right, I haven't got time to deal with this, there are customers out there waiting. Tani, get rid of that disgusting jumper, put your jacket on and relieve Simon. You, young lady, give me your phone. No buts! And get yourself to bed.'

Adrianna stamped upstairs, kicked her bedroom door open and flung herself on the bed. No-one cared, no-one bloody cared. She ripped her headband off and flung that on the floor. She lay looking up at the ceiling. Her parents had no idea what it was like. How could they? Stuck in this disgusting café they called a restaurant day after bloody day, year after bloody year. Forcing her to do crap jobs nobody else wanted. Did she look like a skivy, did she? She dragged her laptop over and opened it, logged on to Facebook.

'Tani, it's time to get the girls from school.'

'What, already?' Thanatos drained his mug of tea and stood up. The last of the lunchtime customers had left, and the boy had just turned on the dishwasher. Thanatos looked at him.

'Y'all right Simon? How you fitting in, getting to know your way round?'

The boy shrugged. He'd been here a week now, and Thanatos had not yet seen him smile. His hair hung over his face in a black wave. Mandy had told him to wear a chef's hat or leave. He'd done neither. Thanatos sighed. Not worth doing a mate a favour. The boy had been suspended from school, six months before his GCSEs, and his father had begged Thanatos to give him something to do before he got himself in trouble.

'Right, I'm off. You want a lift home, Simon?'

Simon gave a brief nod and they went out the back and clambered into the Audi. There was birdshit all over the windscreen and Thanatos swore as he turned on the wipers. They drove along Northdown Road and turned towards St Peter's, Thanatos searching for something to say to the boy. The traffic was backing up already.

'So, there any chance of you going back to school then?'

The 'dunno' from the slight figure at his side, with the black forelock of hair, was just about audible.

'Not too late, Simon, never too late.'

He felt the boy shrug beside him.

'So, how you getting on with the missus then? She done your ears in yet?' Thanatos knew he was being disloyal, but thought what the heck.

An almost incoherent rumble came from the passenger at his side.

'What's that? Sorry mate, didn't hear you.'

'Said, she's awright.'

'Oh!' Well that was good, extremely good in fact. Mandy had had a lot of staff come and go.

'Well, y'know it ain't brain science but it'll do for now, right?'

'I guess.'

'So how's your dad, then?'

'S'awright. This is fine 'ere. Ta.'

Thanatos pulled in by the side of the road, and watched Simon clamber out.

'See ya tomorrow then…?'

'Yeah, tarra.'

He found himself smiling as he pulled away. What the heck.

He pulled up outside the convent by the bus stop. He was early. Through his mirror he could see the usual cavalry start to circle, looking for a parking space. There was the cow from the building society - green hair, purple car, straight on the yellow lines. Didn't give a toss. One of these days he was gonna take a photo of her on his phone, send it in to the local. Now came the mouthy one with the 4x4, she could be a bingo caller with a gob that big. Next the weirdo with the cycling shorts on his bike. Nuff said. Thanatos yawned, watching the parents appear like them blinking animals in Noah's Ark, one by one, two by two. He hated waiting outside schools, hated it. Year in, year out … he was glad the girls were growing up. He wound down the window and lit a fag. The image of the cigar roller came into his head again, her lips red and full, her bare arms rounded, the dampness under her armpit …

'Hi Daddy!' Chloe hauled him back from Havana. She

climbed in the front seat and reached for the seat belt.

'You'd better put that cigarette out right now or Mummy will smell it on my clothes and know. Plus I've told you before that a high percentage of innocent children suffer from passive smoking.'

Thanatos groaned and started the car, attempting to pull out the same time as the Loop bus came swooping round the corner. He found himself mouthing obscenities, aware of Chloe watching him out of the corner of his eye, raising her eyebrows like some Egyptian Queen.

He headed for Ramsgate and daughter number two, who came strolling out of the grammar school like she had all the time in the world, a crowd of boys around her like honeybees. Thanatos drummed his fingers on the steering wheel.

'Daddy, you really need to calm down,' Chloe said. 'Angela's social life is extremely important to her sense of personal identity. Fifteen is an awesome age and tremendously daunting.'

Thanatos turned to look at his daughter beside him, just to make sure it *was* his ten-year old who had climbed into the car back in Broadstairs, and not some shrunken philosopher. She looked back at him open-faced. 'Who d'you think you are, you pint-sized ankle biter?'

'Your youngest and brightest daughter,' she answered swiftly, '*despite* all my genetic setbacks!'

Although he could feel his jaw wanting to drop, Thanatos found himself smiling. Amanda always said Chloe was rightly named. She was eating encyclopaedias by the age of three and putting her oar in wiv Ophra and Jeremy Kyle by six; now it was computers, nature and science programmes.

'Oh is that right?' he said. 'And *whose* genes is it exactly that makes you such a clever-clogs? 'Ow exactly do you think you do so well at school?'

'My own efforts,' she said brightly. 'Attitude, application and dedication. *I* am the one who will make this family proud, wait and see! Adrianna…' she paused, 'Adrianna is going through a … crisis of identity. She is old in body but young in spirit … hmm, a bit like Margate really, not quite sure who she is, who she's to become. Angela now – she's esta … establishing her identity. The second child always has issues … that's why she and Adie fight so much, *and* she and Mum! But, she is quite beautiful, my sister, and a little bit bright too, and a little bit, um … I dunno, not posh exactly but…'

'Full of 'erself!' Thanatos chipped in.

'No, Daddy, self-contained and gracious. Yes, that's it; Angela is gracious. A bit like Ramsgate used to be … we've been studying its history at school and Ramsgate was very posh you know! Though,' she wrinkled her nose and looked through the car window at the dog mess on the pavement, 'you wouldn't think it now would you?'

'And you, my little clever puss, who're you?' Her father asked, amused.

'Well, that's to be seen. I'm still developing aren't I?'

The back door opened suddenly, and Angela slipped in. 'Why does *she* always get to sit in the front?' she said.

'That's life,' Chloe replied, 'tough, get used to it.'

All hell broke loose when they got in. Mandy had found two of her plates cracked in the dishwasher, and as soon as Thanatos broke through the door she rounded on him. Doing a mate a favour? He's blinking bloody useless! No wonder he got chucked out of school! They were all the bleeding same! It was time Tani got more businesslike, all these favours were going to put them out of business. 'Look around you,' she said. 'You think you can make a living running a two-bit café?'

She was wiping down the worktops as she ranted, spraying Flash like there was no tomorrow. Twenty years! Twenty years she'd put her all in. Good when they started, she'd give him that. Helping out on a Saturday, and his dad was a hard worker, give him that. Place spick and span and full of important people. And, sure, they had a good little business for a while, got the girls in the convent and had one or two nice holidays. But what'd it come to, what'd it come to now? One daughter a waste of space, the other too full of 'erself to even bring her friends home!

Tani stood back and let her rant, nodding to Chloe to go upstairs. Mand got like this sometimes, maybe it was that woman's change business or something. He didn't know. Best he keep schtum and let her calm down, then maybe take her to the pictures or something. That'll cheer her up; what was that new film she'd been on about? In the meantime he could go down in the cellar and check out those old photos; you never know do you?

He never knew what made him slip down the cellar stairs, whether he tripped, or if it was that sudden pain in his chest. One minute there he was, reaching for the light switch, the next his feet gave way and he was falling, his head coming to rest at an odd angle on the stone floor. His last thoughts, as his wife's voice still ranted away upstairs, were not oddly of her, or the girls, his Cuban fantasy or even whether the photos were worth anything; instead just a flash of himself and his dad on Margate beach on the feast of Epiphany taking part in the blessing of the waters and then another: himself in his old primary school in Muswell Hill and the sampler on the wall: *In the midst of Life there is Death.*

At the funeral, everyone and anyone commented on how well the family stood together, smart black dresses from Debenhams, Adrianna with her little bow, Mandy in a hat with a tuft of black net, Angela with a sisterly arm around Chloe. A little black quartet in Margate Cemetery: a spit away from the fancy Sanger memorial with the sad horse, his head hanging down, his veins prominent. In the trees the birds held fire.

Clyde the Calypsonian

'You know how easy it was to get black babies back then?' Ivy wiped her hands on the tea towel as she moved around the kitchen, stepping over Clyde's long legs splayed out under the table.

'They were crying out for foster parents then; crying out, I tell you. Nobody dint want coloured children, they land up in children's homes all round the country. Me and your dad was one of the first to foster them. Nancy had three or four before Leanne. The first one's mother came back and got him, just as he was settling down, nearly seven he was, started school. Mother turned up out of the blue – said she'd sorted herself out and took him off to Birmingham. Nancy never heard another word. Then she had the twins and baby Leanne; twins were a handful, white mother didn't want to know, took herself off back somewhere up north so Nancy said. You should have heard the shit Nancy used to get from some of those old people in the bungalows, nasty-minded lot them.

'Golliwogs' they used to call the poor little mites, standing there by the bus stop on a Thursday, pension day, sniffing. Not everybody mind, a lot of people was tickled pink by them, Leanne in particular so pretty-pretty with them big eyes and hair like a pom-pom with pink ribbon. Some aunty of the twins turned up when they was thirteen, ten years, ten years after Nancy raise them, teach them manners, feed them, clothe them. Mummy Nancy, they used to call her, Mummy Nancy. Broke her heart. But at least she still got Leanne. Nice girl Leanne. Story was her mother come from round here somewhere, father some Negro American airman. Turned out all right though. Shame you and her…' She paused, staring out the kitchen window at a blackbird on the washing line.

'Of course some people did it for the money. See them down the town pushing new pushchairs and driving fancy cars. But Nancy wasn't like that. Them twins was growing to be real nice boys, I tell you. When the aunty turn up with photographs and all kinds of official papers, Nancy didn't have a leg to stand on, she sat right here at this kitchen table and cried how she wish she had adopted them while she had the chance. Next thing I know, the boys fly out to Nigeria. What the hell they know 'bout Nigeria?' She turned to face Clyde then. Coffee mug in hand, he looked up and her and sighed.

'Well, Ma…'

'You ever think about your real Ma?' she asked suddenly.

Clyde shifted uncertainly. His hand stretched upwards and scratched his head. 'Well I can't lie and say I never…'

'But you was happy, wasn't you, Clyde? With me and you Pa? We tell you all we knew, you was happy enough with that, wasn't you?'

Clyde ran his fingers over the baby dreads. 'Ma, you and Pa always did the best for me, you know I 'preciate everything. And course when I find out Trinidad was my roots I was cool with that.'

'Yes, who can forget you and your calypso music blasting through you bedroom door! But I ain't looking for no gratitude, Clyde. That's why I can't understand this nonsense about your culture. You always know you was a black boy, I never told you you was white did I?'

She pointed to the newspaper laying open on the table: 'New Rules For Fostering Black Children.'

'You believe me and your Pa teach you not to care about black people?'

'No Ma. That not what it's about. They only trying to match children with parents from a similar ethnicity that's all.'

'Ethnicity? All? After all the years of you living here with Pa and me who were both white all them years ago and still the same colour now, how they can suddenly turn around and say we can't foster your child, *our grandchild,* because he needs to grow up with 'regard to his culture'! You tell me Clyde, what strangers can give your child that I can't, just because they are the same colour?'

'Look Ma, don't upset yourself. Dante is being fostered in Hackney because it's where his mother people are, he's at school already and yes, Hackney is more multi-cultural, and yes he will learn more about Marcus Garvey and Martin Luther King there than he would at Newington!'

'But doesn't the time he's spent with me matter? Who looked after Dante since Shireen get sick? I was good enough then wasn't I? And who are these people? His mother's people? What? Uncles he knows nothing about? They didn't even put their hand up! These are strangers, strangers with nothing in common with your son except the colour of his skin!'

Clyde stood up suddenly and pushed back his chair.

'Well, that's what you don't understand! What none of you understand! Do you not know the significance of colour, Ma? Are you that blind? It's easy for you, isn't it! No-one stares at you because of the colour of your skin, Ma! That's what we have to live with, day in, day out in a place like this where me and Leanne were the only "tar-babies!" Did you pay any attention to the news about the Brixton Riots, Ma? Or do you think it don't apply to you? Get real for Chrissake, there's a world out there, and it's nastier and more insidious than anything you could ever imagine outside this "Garden of Kent"!'

He walked out the kitchen door then, heading for the back gate, leaving Ivy, mouth open, staring after him.

Clyde walked along the alleyway behind the council houses. Some were obscured from vision, large trees and the backs of sheds, padlocked gates. Others swung open, trailed sagging wire fences, well-tended veg plots, broken bikes and toys. He didn't want to be rude to Ivy. She was the only mother he had. This was where he'd spent a large part of his life, this estate with its wheat and its chaff. What was that line from Marley, "old pirates … sold I to the merchant ships…"

He walked out along the Newington Road thinking about the conversation he'd just had. He knew he had much to be grateful for; his first memory was of sitting on Ramsgate Sands making sandcastles; running to the water's edge with his little yellow bucket and wandering back, careful not to spill it. Ivy still had that old thing, pictures of seahorses all round. He remembered nothing before that; only knew what he had been told, his natural mother depositing him in a children's home. On and off through the years he'd thought about tracing her, but never acted on it. Ivy had told him of the pictures in the papers back then, babies and children in ones and twos, their large eyes and pleading faces begging for new mums and dads. Ivy and Trevor hadn't been able to have children. Trevor worked in the pits at Betteshanger, and Ivy at Hornby's, packing toy trains. Those faces had tugged at her heartstrings, Ivy would say. What was she doing packing toy trains all day when she could be giving a poor child a proper home? Trevor was an easy-going man; it hadn't taken much to persuade him.

Clyde remembered the working men's clubs, the social occasions when they'd take Clyde along, the bingo games, the singers and comedians up on stage. He didn't remember any outright racism; that came later, from strangers; what he remembered was learning how to laugh. It was only later he would learn what that laughter consisted of, an innate racism born out of ignorance. 'Ay Clyde when you leave school you come down the pits wi' us, mate, you won't know difference!'

He remembered the first time he saw the comedian Charlie Williams on telly, and Lenny Henry. They all laughed first at themselves. Without knowing he'd slipped into being like that himself. The comedian, the boy at the back of the class larking about. He earned his cap at primary school, thrown out of a relatively protected environment of Ivy and the women who sat round her kitchen table drinking tea, their hard voices and rough laughter softening when he entered the room with a cut knee or a request for a jam sandwich.

At school, his world had widened to include the sons of butchers and greengrocers, market traders and taxi drivers, all resting their vision of the world that impacted on them through TV programmes like *Love Thy Neighbour* on their children. He'd never forget the name-calling, slung like arrows round the schoolyard walls and finding their mark on a little boy only then realising his skin was darker than theirs, and that for some reason it mattered.

That's when the Irish boys came into play, Drake and Errol Donoghue, one minute laying into him same as the others, the next lining up by him, fists tight like boxers facing the pack with faces hard as nuts and feet as light as ballet dancers. Three monkeys they called them, wild as foxes but with antics that made the teachers fond of them.

As Clyde grew older, more battles had to be faced, and many a fight was fought on the streets of the council estate, battles of words from hard-faced old men leaning on gateposts, and unemployed young men moving out from school to a life of unemployment.

The Irish boys, named after Hollywood stars in black and white films watched religiously by their mother on Saturday afternoons, stuck by Clyde, deflecting bottles and fists with a wildness akin to Connemara and the American West. Drake and Errol and their older brother Jamie were the hard nuts of Ramsgate, moving on from kicking a football round the rec to an easy relationship with public houses, taking Clyde along with them.

Music was the gel. Clyde the entertainer became the Ramsgate representative for Bob Marley and James Brown, coolness, an ambassador of blackness. 'Hey Clyde, you should know this, man. Hey Clyde show us how to dance reggae.' His small universe was as fragile as a spider's web. Over in a Margate nightclub with coach-loads of outsiders from other parts of Kent, skinheads from Dartford, Dover or Chatham, things were different. 'Is that a coon on the dance floor? Hey it's Charlie Williams' little brother!' Many an evening ended with fights. Fists, knives, chains. One Bank Holiday it was mayhem, Margate swimming with bikers looking for a fight, Black Marias screaming outside Dreamland and pulling in punters by the dozen on charges ranging from possessing cannabis to assault with a deadly weapon.

Then that other Bank Holiday Monday, an August bright and full of sunshine, ushering a trail of day-trippers down to the seaside, cars streaming down the M2, hired coaches and trains from which families poured out with pushchairs, rolled-up beachmats, hampers of food and drink streaming down the High Streets and promenades of Ramsgate, Broadstairs and Margate. Clyde had been in the Royal pub on Ramsgate Harbour with the boys, standing on the pavement with full glasses of lager, watching the trail of day-trippers head for the beach. A coachload of black Londoners spilling out by the harbour, a ghetto blaster held high on tall shoulders.

Drake had nudged Clyde in the ribs: 'Watcher, mate, your cousins are in!'

They'd all laughed, watching a matronly figure usher the party past the marina and behind Peggy Sue's. Soon the smell of fried chicken and goat curry, heated up on a Campingaz stove, rose into a Ramsgate air more used to fish and chips.

The music and the smell had lured the boys to the beach; they stripped off to trunks and rushed into the cold waters of the Channel. That's where he'd seen her, standing by the shoreline in a red and white swimsuit.

In later times he'd wonder what direction his life might have changed if he hadn't met Shireen. How ignorant he would have remained of the wide sweep of his own identity, a history of which, so far, he had barely scratched the surface. Seated in a front room in Hackney face to face with elders and young men who eyed him suspiciously he had felt even more a stranger. Shireen's father could not believe he didn't know who Marcus Garvey was, or Rosa Parks. They shook their heads in disbelief, although this was mildly redressed by his knowledge of Lord Invader and Mighty Sparrow. Clyde didn't reveal his source, pirate radio.

Over the following months, Ivy, borrowing the phone from the corner shop to find out what was going on, found herself talking to a son who not only sounded different, but *was* different. 'No I'm not ready to come home, Ivy.' Ivy, he had called her Ivy.

Clyde was getting an education that had not featured on the syllabus at Holy Cross High School. Sam Selvon's *The Lonely Londoners*; Trinidad's Black Power Revolution in 1970; Malcolm X; Marcus Garvey; Martin Luther King; the poet Linton Kwesi Johnson, the black consciousness newspaper, *Race Today*... Ivy would have fainted if she'd witnessed the demonstration that her son got caught up with in Brixton, a peaceful event against Racism and the Suss laws, which had ended up with police horses and water cannon. When she did get a phone call it was to say that he and Shireen had had a baby, but Shireen had taken ill, and her parents could not help out. It was a broken man that came back to Newington and stood there on the doorstep with a baby. Shireen had sickle cell disease, and was on a kidney machine. Her parents were caring for her and were too distraught to care for a baby too.

Clyde moved back in part-time with Ivy and Trevor, for whom the crying of a baby momentarily took them back to 1965, when it was Clyde who bawled for attention, and Clyde's diapers danced on the washing line. But this little boy was Dante, Clyde's son. Clyde was up and down to Hackney each week, trying to be there for Shireen, lending her parents a hand. It was the stress of this and the inability that led to dealing. That and the death of Jamie Donoghue, the bad man of Ramsgate, the deflector of racist abuse against Clyde since primary school.

After his funeral, Clyde sat with Drake and Errol in The Royal Standard, heads bowed in shock. How had death come so suddenly to someone so young and vibrant? You expect the soldier to die in battle, go down guns blazing like those Westerns his mother watched, Gary Cooper in a shootout. You didn't expect a warrior to choke to death in a fancy restaurant.

Clyde held that moment as the one of his fall. Jamie dead, Shireen fading away in Hackney, Dante growing round-eyed with the confusion. The daily newspapers brought the politicisation of black youth even to Thanet, as if Clyde needed any new reason to be looked at suspiciously if he boarded a bus or a train. Money was tight. He upped his game with dealing, the boys pointing out how easy it was the coming and going between London and Thanet. But he was no Buffalo Soldier. He got six months in Brixton. If he wanted any more education he got it. The piss taken out of him to be caught with a few grams of hash. Being raised by a white woman. Living in the land of Babylon. He told himself he was not political. But Shireen's Uncle Franklin, one of those who had laughed at his ignorance of Black History, was waiting for him when he was released. 'You think you could be a black man in this country and not be political? You're a blasted fool.'

He headed for Newington Road now and waited for the bus. There was a young woman there with a twin push-chair. Clyde didn't realise who it was until she spoke.

'Well yo get so big up now Clyde you ain't got time for your old friends?'

It was Leanne. She turned aside and blew smoke from her cigarette into the concrete air. One of the kids was whingeing.

'O shit, Leanne, sorry girl, didn't know it was you. Thoughts far and all that.'

'Haven't seen you round for ages. You living in the smoke now, aintcha?'

'Man I'm all over the place, you heard about Shireen?'

'Yeah, sorry, must be tough for you. I seen your mum Ivy with your little boy.'

'Yeah yeah…'

'*Well* proud of him she was… '

'Yeah, well, you know they're getting on, plus this ain't the right environment for him now you know.'

'No, how d'you mean, we turned out alright didn't we?'

'Come on, Leanne, how can you say that, girl? You remember the names we used to get called? I remember me and the boys had to rescue you more than once from those

109

bastards down Whitehall Road!'

'Yeah, I remember Jamie rearranging one of their faces!' She laughed and stubbed her cigarette out on the ground. 'Yeah it was tough, but then we was the only ones, wasn't we? You with your mystery parents and me with some American airman for a dad! But I don't feel hard done by; at least we didn't end up in no children's home! If anything,' she paused, 'if anything I feel like a pioneer.'

Clyde tried to change the subject. Trust her and Ivy to confuse the issue. 'So these your two yeah?'

'I got another boy, Curtis; he's seven. Just started Scouts. He'll be in the Carnival next Sunday, you around?'

'What, Ramsgate Carnival?' He laughed and shook his head. 'You ever been to Notting Hill, Leanne?'

'Seen it on telly, why?'

'Well, that's what you call a Carnival, girl! Our people playing mas, celebrating our roots! Girl you don't know nothing till you sweat and dance with black people!'

'Clyde, I know where my roots are man.' She waved her arm in a semi-circle in the air, and Clyde's eyes followed, resting on the fish and chip shop, the newsagents, and the old man shuffling across the road. He sucked his teeth and shook his head.

'Girl, you need some serious information! You think this is your roots?' He laughed. He looked at her standing there in a pair of cut off jeans, T-shirt, Levi jacket. A young black woman with calm, brown, unquestioning eyes. Her twins looked up at him. For the first time he noticed they weren't black, they had coffee-coloured skin and soft unruly curls. She drew another circle in the air, from her heart then round the pushchair.

Heading for Ramsgate Station later, his hands wandered over his head, the new dreadlocks growing, the start of a new identity. The Calypsonians kept cussing. Marley went down fighting. He thought of Drake and Errol, both caught up in a life that had no history of substance, the joy gone out of them, cancer, drugs and violence eating them up. He wasn't going to let that happen to him. He might not have known who his real mother was, England was his motherland; he might have a lot to be angry about, to rebel against, but he also had a lot to thank her for. In the row about Dante, he had never got round to telling Ivy his news, that he'd enrolled to study law at Goldsmiths. Tonight, when he got home, he would ring her, tell her he loved her. Maybe they could even sort something out about Dante. He thought about Leanne and her sense of self. Maybe she had a point. That Carnival now … man! imagine if he could bring Notting Hill to Margate! You never know, do you, where it might all lead. After all, where did he learn about the Mighty Sparrow? Radio Caroline, a pirate ship! "Old pirates, yes, they rob I, sold I to the merchant ships…"

Talking Books

'Well of course Jean Rhys means to illuminate the gaps in Bronte's novel...'

'I quite disagree. This isn't a novel about individual circumstance ... it's the writer making a political statement.'

'What do *you* think, Renata?'

'Me? About what?' The two previous speakers, Mandy and Peggy, laughed.

'Wake up, Renata! We're discussing *The Wide Sargasso Sea*. Jean Rhys? You did read it, didn't you?'

Renata's hands flustered in her lap. 'No, sorry, well I've started it...'

'Oh dear, I thought we'd all agreed to make an effort to come with the books read?' Mandy's eyes ran over the group.

'I've seen the film!' Vanessa volunteered. She adjusted her large frame on the narrow chair.

'I ... it's just that my husband's still off work and I just don't seem to find the time,' Renata continued.

Mandy smiled at her benevolently. 'Don't worry, dear, just listen … and the film has something to say too, so we can return to that later.'

'Hello everyone, sorry I'm late.' Joseph appeared from behind one of the bookshelves, Tesco's Bag For Life in hand. He relieved himself of his jacket and joined the circle, settling himself in one of the empty chairs. He looked around, offering a thin nervous smile as he foraged in his bag and pulled out his book.

'Sorry, the Loop buses are all over the place today … missed one and had to wait thirty minutes for another.'

'They're supposed to run every fifteen minutes.' This from Minty, the youngest in the group.

'Yeah, right!' Verma rolled her eyes upwards. 'Just once, just once I get the bus. No More. My daughter don't drop me, I don't come.' She crossed her arms across her chest decisively.

'Verma, it would be interesting to hear your viewpoint, seeing that you aren't as well acquainted, and therefore influenced, with and by *Jane Eyre* as most of us are? What is your opinion of the book?'

'Oh I like, I like very much! I read and don't put down. Very nice book.' Her smile was wide as she nodded enthusiastically.

'What *exactly* did you like about it, Verma? For instance, is it different from any other book you've read before?'

'Different? No, not so much different, I read many many books about love, you know.'

'Ah, so you think this is a story about love? That's interesting.'

'I beg your pardon,' Joseph put his hand up hesitantly.

He looked at Verma apologetically. 'Sorry, Verma, I hope you don't mind if I disagree.'

'No, no,' she waved her fingers, gold rings flashing.

'I don't think this is a story about love at all,' he said

earnestly. Several Post-it notes protruded from the book in his hand. 'This is an act of vengeance. A literary act of vengeance.'

Confusion swiftly crossed everyone's features. They waited. He swallowed nervously, his Adam's apple loose under his skin. 'Jean Rhys, the writer, was a very unhappy woman, I … er … have been reading some background information, and her life itself reads like a novel. And in fact most of her novels were heavily influenced by her life. It's a case of art reflecting life, so to speak.'

'Don't really get you, Joseph,' Mandy said slowly, 'as I don't think any of us have read much beyond the book we're at a bit of a disadvantage.'

'Sorry, yes, I mean … what I'm trying to say is that she, the writer, is Antoinette the character, is a woman crossed in love, yes, but as the writer she creates the power she did not have in reality in early 20th Century Europe…'

'So it is a book about power, not love?' Verma asked.

'What did you mean when you said it was literary … literary…?' Minty asked.

'Vengeance. Ah yes, well it has to go back to *Jane Eyre* … sorry, Verma, I know you didn't study it in Ukraine … but let us ask ourselves this: if Jean Rhys had not been a Creole woman, would she have been able to or in fact choose to write *The Wide Sargasso Sea?*'

'Oh, but this is hypothetical. We have spoken before about this problem,' Peggy said. 'It doesn't matter why someone writes a book, surely? Shouldn't the book be a thing of itself?'

Renata put her hand up and then dropped it back in her lap.

'I think the argument, no, let me rephrase that, the *discussion* about a writer's reasons for writing is a whole argument in itself,' Mandy said. 'However it does play a part, and I personally think it is very relevant in this case.'

'Why in this case, Mandy?' Vanessa asked.

'Because we are discussing a book that, although it is written in English and has English connections, is not really English, is it?'

'Rochester is English!' Peggy said.

'Lots of people in it are English.' Minty added.

'But it doesn't feel English, does it?' Mandy asked.

'Is that because the landscape features so much? That flamboyant, stifling, seductive and overwhelming almost *alien* landscape…?' Joseph sat forward in his seat.

'Yes, not exactly Margate is it?' Minty laughed. 'I can't see anyone setting a story of passion and love in Margate! Where would it take place, Palm Bay car park?'

'Don't laugh, Minty! Didn't you see the film with David Tennant in it? There was film crews all ova the place, even the council offices!' said Vanessa.

'There wasn't all English people in it was there? Didn't they have one about a Thai bride?' Minty asked.

Mandy raised both hands, the cue for silence.

'Reading Group, we are getting off the subject. The subject is *The Wide Sargasso Sea*, remember?'

'Oh I dunno, Mand,' Peggy said, 'you was the one said it wasn't English!'

'Well I thought that Joseph was interesting; what he said about landscape,' Verma offered.

'Yes, yes, we agree on that, Verma! The landscape is almost a character in itself, it has a strong personality, and also the character viewpoint! Antoinette, and the narrow, almost claustrophobic world she inhabits…' Joseph offered enthusiastically.

'…which Rochester, the cold Englishman enters!' Peggy added.

'I haven't read it all, but the film does make it seem like it is a love story,' Renata said quietly.

'The film has little or no bearing to the book,' Joseph said.

'Films are so disappointing, once you've read the book,

aren't they? I saw *The Hunger Games* on DVD recently and though it was good, it really wasn't as good as the book at all!' Peggy said.

'That was a well good book that was!' said Minty. 'I nabbed it off my little brother and couldn't put it down! Hey why don't we put that on the list to read?'

'It's a children's book, isn't it?' asked Verma.

'So what? Let's think about how many adults read Harry Potter!' Minty retorted.

'Well we're a very democratic group, so I don't see a problem with considering it for the future. To return to *Wide Sargasso Sea…*' Mandy began assertively.

'Sorry Joseph, can I just say … it's just that I just had a thought: my little brother normally don't read anything. Always on the computer, you know what they're like! Well anyway he liked them *Hunger Games* books so much he read 'em all! And that's how I got hold of it too! But the books were just like a video game you know, and I was just wondering if we find it hard to read books that are, like, outside our experience?'

Many of the group nodded at that. Some commented on the fact that it was really hard to get into some books whilst others said for them it was like reading was like armchair travelling, they got to encounter the world.

At break some of them made for the coffee machine, a recent feature of the library.

'Oh, this is nice now, this library,' Verma said to Minty. 'You know it was so different in Ukraine! No speaking, old, cold rooms. I never went to library, not me!'

'Do you like coming to the group, Verma?'

'Oh yes, for me it give me chance to meet and talk. I know I not very clever but I enjoy anyway.'

'Oh, don't say that Verma! You're way cleverer than me! I never sit no exams or nothing, I had a baby when I was fifteen.'

'You have a baby? Oh goodness me, what you have? You married?'

'A little boy, yeah, Corey. He's really cute. No, I live with Mum and Dad, and I do want to do something but I don't know what, so I thought I'd start with this. I always liked reading at school.'

Joseph was having a quiet word with Mandy. 'Sorry, Mandy, I know you're trying your best, but it's difficult to get a real conversation going isn't it?'

'You're telling me! Sometimes I feel like a schoolteacher again! Thing is not to take it too seriously. For many people it's a social thing, the group, though they like to think it keeps their brains ticking. You're looking a bit stressed, Joseph, are you all right?'

'Yes, yes, no, really, it's just that … it's just that I was a bit worried by your comment about Englishness. I mean I know you didn't mean anything by it, it's just that I wondered how Verma for example, might take it…'

'I beg your pardon? What on earth do you mean? I thought we had quite a good little discussion about that?'

'Sorry, sorry, Mandy, never mind me…'

'Right then, are we all back and raring for round two? Before we start, would everyone mind if we just cleared up a few things? No? Right then! Talking about books can be quite a passionate activity! I just wondered if everyone feels okay, not miffed about anything? Good! We're all adults here, and I'm sure we all respect each other's views. Now this novel is a very challenging one, and we haven't quite defined it as yet. I know from my experience of teaching, though of course I've been retired a while now, that everyone will have their own opinions. So, so far we have had some opinions that the book is about love, someone said power, and someone else said landscape. I personally am intrigued by Joseph's comment about it being an act of literary vengeance. I haven't heard that before! So I thought we could just ask Joseph to explain a little more about that, if he doesn't mind?'

Joseph had his head down, flicking through the pages, re-adjusting the Post-it notes. 'Um ah, okay, sorry, and thanks, Mandy.' He cleared his throat. 'What I meant, and this is borne by some background knowledge, knowing a bit more about the writer and her other works, was the *possibility* that because of her circumstances of being someone from the Caribbean, and having some knowledge of slavery and our own country's involvement in that unsavoury practice, could Rhys, a woman disempowered, disastrous relationships, etc, etc, have in her mind blamed English history and culture for her circumstances, and saw in *Jane Eyre* a window through which she could, imaginatively of course, seek blame and give it force through the art of writing? After all in *Jane Eyre* the madwoman in the attic is from the West Indies and we do not get to hear her side of the story in Bronte's book do we? I'm not saying I do not like the book, or agree it has significance. I just propose the theory that this is a form of vengeance for the sins of our forefathers?'

His voice faded away in the silence. In the background, traffic rolled past in Cecil Square. Behind the bookcases, the unemployed stared at computers. A child was grizzling in the children's section.

Minty spoke. 'I read somewhere that *The Hunger Games* was based on Greek myths. I can't remember any from school though.'

'I thought it was interesting the way the book was divided into three parts. You get to see things from different perspectives,' Peggy said.

'Well, I think it would be a very sad thing for anyone claiming to be a writer to sit down and contemplate any sort of vengeance, literary or otherwise,' Vanessa said huffily.

'Yeah, seems petty don't it? Like making up stories just 'cos someone else did,' said Minty.

Verma coughed and said, 'You know, in some cultures they don't like people, usually girls, to learn to read?'

'Why on earth not? Sounds very silly to me,' said Renata, flicking through the book.

'Probably because everyone would end up arguing like us!' Peggy laughed.

'Naw, we ain't arguing. I think it's dead interesting!' Minty said.

'Yes, it's made me want to persevere with reading it now,' said Renata.

'Well ladies, and gentleman … my goodness, time's caught up with us already! You know I have a feeling we could carry on talking all day! Haha! As if we haven't got lives to lead! Anyway, it's been wonderful as usual, thank you for all your contributions. Next time we've got Jeffrey Archer, let's all try and read it and come with questions and ideas. Okay?'

'Thanks, Mandy.'

'Thanks, Mand, see you everyone.'

'Cheers.'

The small bout of clapping didn't go unheard by the librarian. She wondered if she should say something. She didn't want to upset anyone but the library did have other users … it was all about accessibility and democracy now … only thing is sometimes they rubbed up rough against each other. She watched the girl Minty edge up alongside the *How To* books. She was sure she went to school with her. Didn't she get pregnant at fifteen? Huh! Okay for some to have the liberty to go to book groups. Not like her, working her ass off, job description constantly changing and now more staff cuts threatened. Typical. She stamped down hard on the book the Russian woman was taking out: *War and Peace*. Christ.

When Benjamin Zephaniah Came to Broadstairs

What, as a Caribbean ex-pat, should an English folk festival mean to her? Veronique, sitting on the promenade at Broadstairs, contemplates this. She has just come from taking her grandchildren to see Benjamin Zephaniah, and they're now eating sausage rolls in the sun. The town jangles around her with its annual marauders – men with blackened faces, girls with wild hair and sticks, the whine and wail of fiddles and squeeze boxes. Baubles glint from the temporary stalls all the way to the Bandstand, the yellow Folk Week colour blazing.

Bleak House, a hotel now, sits perched on the cliff top. The beach below swarms with visitors; the screeches of children rising like the seagulls, permeating the orchestrated air. Behind her, the garden of the Albion Hotel is packed with lunchtime punters resting their bare arms on glass and chrome. She remembers the old straggling hedge, the weather-worn tables, the children's bare legs crossed on the bleached grass, the Red Arrows dipping and screaming in the skies above.

Rooks' sausage rolls in paper bags, the pigeon at her feet, pecking. So many years, crumbling: from her own babies in pushchairs, her young girl's breasts, her brown legs; now these boisterous, sprouting grandchildren.

The festival had exploded over the last thirty years, from a small gathering in Pierremont Park. Then, folk dancers and Morris sides clumped on wooden boards to an audience sat on tree stumps drinking cider from the off licence. She had countless photos of her children and the festival growing. Chasing cousins and school friends round on the stage. At the Bandstand, with Clarence the dragon. In painted faces. With ice-creams. Maypole dancing. At the Torchlight Procession. Some of their faces broke through the years, appeared wearing onesies in Tesco, arrived in envelopes from New Zealand and America. She kept them in yellow boxes under her bed.

She thought of some of the useless skills she had acquired over the years - drumming, storytelling, clog-dancing. Her purchases were time machines all over the house – Morris the ceramic cat whose tail hung neatly over the dresser, the harmonica still in its' box, the tin whistle, the bodhran that exploded in the heat of the conservatory. The djembes bought at great expense, one flown in especially from Ghana to Manston airport, the other from the Senegalese, Ali, in the shop on Albion Road (long gone now). She had been at her most extrovert with those. Cared not for any neighbours who might not have appreciated her passion for the rooted sound of Africa. Even when her teenagers came home and said, 'Mum, I could hear you playing that flipping drum from the top of the road!' Neither shame nor modesty had affected her newly discovered sense of self.

She looks at families now, the visitors; pitying the tiredness, the dragging feet, the toddlers crying, the dropped ice creams. She thinks of the long drag from the campsite, their endless steps up and along the beach, laden with buckets and spades, the parents trying to fit in activities for everyone. So much choice now – circus skills, drama workshops...

She wouldn't fancy taking any of hers into the cramped pubs now. Everything was once so laid back ... nodding their heads to the violins, tapping their feet to the bodhrans, roaring to choruses of 'Wild Rover', the children side by side. Many's the night she and her husband almost drowned in pints of resentment on who got to take the kids back home whilst the other stayed out for the *craic,* the camaraderie, music pouring out from the pubs, feeding the atmosphere, this seven days of carnival.

Tie-dyed T-shirts and bright skirts float by, embroidered waistcoats and Tyrolean hats. The poet who always wore purple. Uncle Adrian, dressed as Aunty Pat.

There were other effects that Folk Week had, which she couldn't tell a living soul. Not even the man she still loved. How could she tell him how hot she felt during the festival, especially when the sun was shining? (Make no mistake, many times rain fell on Clarence, emptied the seats around the Bandstand, dampened the sheen of the parakeets' phosphorescent plumage.) No. The kind of hot was the rush of lust that forged her every step, her every lounging moment, leaning back on her arms, watching the array of colour like flags, young men in Bermuda shorts, bare chests with medallions, the straps of guitars, tight jeans, day-old beards, rough tumbled heads of hair. Year after year the Gods returned, bringing their Bacchanalian bodies of promise, their utterances of poetry written in crofts, on wild mountainsides, their hardened fingers moulded to guitars and violins. She imagined sex with them in the Albion Hotel; she imagined sex with them on the beach at night under the pier where the young boys dived. She imagined slipping into their campervans or 2CVs and heading up the M2 for a life where music, sex and poetry blended smoothly with an isolated farmhouse and rock concerts in Madrid.

These passions remained as the years passed, she didn't know if her involvement, the useless activities she took part in was because of them, or despite them. At one level she felt herself growing as a person, and all the new-age talk that accompanied this transformation, all the incense sticks and yoga, wholefood and buying British, becoming British, all became part of the same thing.

By the time Benjamin Zephaniah came to the festival, she had grown as large as Mother Sally, a giant sculptured Caribbean head seen so frequently now as part of British festivals. She had grown from a seed transplanted from the old world to the new and back again. She could debate academically the value of Chinua Achebe's *Things Fall Apart,* Kamau Brathwaite as a Caribbean griot, and carried Bessie Head, Salif Keita and Mandela to bed with her every night. The advent of World Music into the festival had been a happy coincidence with her academic study as a mature student. Zimbawean choirs, Mongolian musicians and Syrian soloists had joined West Country mandolin players and Cornish sea-shanty singers into the new definition of folk which kept on evolving, becoming 'cool' through the music of Mumford and Sons and Seth Lakeman. The pubs got busier. A marquee erected. Whilst her children grew up unconfused and British, ashamed of her gauche drumming, dismissive of Clarence, focused on Nike trainers, tested their freedom to smoke and use bad language, and had no idea what they wanted to do, she thumbed through a battered copy of Ntozake Shangwe's *For colored girls who have considered suicide when the rainbow is enuf...* at the Charles Dickens' boot fair.

She had felt it her duty to usher her grandchildren in to hear the poet, the poet whose words had already informed her years since, a black man whose own journey had had a rickety start, but now who could joke about turkeys and command a world tour. But in that room full of mothers and children, teachers and classroom assistants, people who had seen him on the telly and came even though they knew nothing about poetry, her grandchildren had sat unmoved, the boys fidgeting, constantly asking the time.

So they sit and eat their sausage rolls on the promenade, and the languages of the world surround them, and fire-eaters surround them, and stiltmen tower above them, and Morris girls bash the hell out of sticks. The evening ahead did not beckon enticingly. Youth and drink had killed the dragon.

Colour, heat and noise swirled around her like a dust-bowl. Suddenly, in the harbour a ship appeared: an India-man, full to the brim with wives for Bombay. Alongside: a steamboat, The Waverley, Edwardian passengers stepping down the gangplank in linen and parasols. Out to sea, a hoy, passengers dispersed at Margate, afraid of the wild Goodwins, sails past with the luggage to Ramsgate. And there, just pulling in to the pier, a sailing ship, bound for the colonies. She could see the faces of those on board as clear as the tar-faced Rochester Morris men – they loomed in her vision as clear as an HDTV – a choir of black men and women all facing her, a sound washing over her in a wave, as strong as a Welsh choir. She felt a strong urge to join them, could see her father amongst them, holding his Hawaiian guitar. But something, someone, was tugging at her sleeve.

Her granddaughter, River.

'Granny,' she says, 'Granny, *I* really liked the poems.'

Her small face peers up at her through a silk of hair. Veronique feels her heart constrict, and she looks up again at the sea. A blue sea, one small white sail, triangular in the distance.

The Mermaid Tour

There was a mermaid on a scooter outside the station. Gary rubbed his eyes twice, hard, with the back of his fist.

'Oi! Gary!' she shouted. He did a quick shufti round to see if it was him she was hailing.

The car park was full. Summertime. Bare-feet, bare-headed, bare-assed. It wasn't only the picnic baskets spilling over. But no one else called Gary stepped up.

'Oi! Gary!' She shouted again. 'Do you wanna ride or what?'

Gary clocked her, carefully this time. Long hair, Adidas top, sunglasses, earpiece and speaker phone. Oh, and tail, tucked in neatly on the scooter plate. The engine was running. Without a word he climbed on. She twiddled the handles with her fingers. For some reason Gary was glad about that: he had no idea how she'd kick-start the engine. He'd had a long journey and couldn't be arsed to work out the machinations of a mermaid on a scooter. He glanced at her hands, though; happy to see they looked normal. Her fingernails were chipped, lime-green nail varnish flaking, and her knuckles were muddy. Bloody hell, he thought, don't tek care of herself, does she? She's either a mechanic or climbed her way out the grotto.

As soon as he settled himself they were off. He got a mouthful of hair as she spun the bike round in the car park. Fine, flyaway, fishy hair it was, blonde. Or it could have been the smell coming in off the beach. It was low tide and he could see the bunched-up seaweed left high and dry on the sand.

'Bit of a pong, that! Do you get a lot of that down here?' he shouted. But the engine was spluttering like a geriatric's cough and she didn't hear him. He tried again, reckoning he should attempt some effort at conversation, but the wind swallowed his words.

She slowed up by the roundabout and turned right along the promenade. She passed him something over her shoulder. It was an earpiece. He grasped it with a wavering hand, the other gripping the underside of his seat firmly. He placed it behind his ear, and almost jumped when he heard her voice, catching sight of her the same time in the wing mirror.

'Do you want the whole works or the quickie?'

He nearly did fall off the bike then. She'd sped up past the clock tower, and was belting it hell for leather up the hill. He clocked the new gallery as she sped past.

'The whole works, of course!'

He caught her eyes again in the mirror. She was smiling. Pulling his leg, weren't she! Got a sense of humour. Especially since she herself didn't have a leg to stand on.

He nearly said 'Baby' after 'full works'. Stopped himself in time. Didn't want to get too familiar. He'd noticed the knuckle-dusters on her fingers. Guess she had to have some form of self-defence, he couldn't see her going fast off the bike on a flipper.

'Right, well that piece of architecture we just passed sits on the site of a real ship, the Ship Inn. Site of many a Friday rockabilly night, just the place to catch your breath when you stagger out pissed. Wind's famous for that here. Tucked away on your right is the Northern Belle, the oldest pub in Margate named after a Yankee ship that went down, used to be The Watermen's Arms. Whole lifeboat crew went down trying to save 'em. Coming up round this corner, now a very attractive block of flats, lies the ghost of The Hippocampo, a nightclub that spanned the history of music from rock, reggae and soul. Reckon that killed it. Confusion. Some used to have a laugh there though. Bet you didn't know the singer from Madness married a Ramsgate girl, didja? On your right another ghost, the famous Butlins. Site of mass entertainment, and dolphinarium. Animals didn't have many rights then.'

She slowed down to point out to Gary the tiny Tom Thumb Theatre, a place, she said, that was worth the effort if and when he had the time.

'A completely different kettle of fish to this,' she said, pointing out the Winter Gardens sprawling against the backdrop of the Channel. Its entrance was framed by an expanse of canna lilies and pink begonias. 'Very grand in its day, of course. You should see the old plans for it, amazing. Me mam saw Gene Pitney there. Twice.' They sped up again; turning left at the junction and following the road round to Palm Bay. Gary spied entrances that seemed to offer cars access to the promenade below, but she didn't use these.

She slowed down by the turn and kept up her patter.

'Used to be an aquarium here. Yeah, you wouldn't think it, would ya? That's where me mam met that bastard she insisted was me dad. They found him washed up at Pegwell some years back, so there's no proving he was. Me dad, I mean.' She laughed, a little crackly laugh over the earpiece. 'Nice place though, by all accounts.'

Gary's eyes were whipped by the salt breeze. They rode the stretch of Palm Bay in silence. She turned right then, speeding past a road stacked with bungalows, and then, in a swift manoeuvre over a main road, they were bumping along on grass. Gary spotted a playground and shut his eyes as a woman hastily swerved her pushchair out the way.

'This is Northdown Park,' his guide informed him cheerily, roaring and weaving round the flowerbeds. 'Site of the famous escaping parakeets who now rule the whole island. Viva! Anything's better than those schizo seagulls!' Next thing they were on tarmac and she indicated what once was a manor house, but she didn't have the faintest what purpose it served except to have weddings now. 'Though I've heard it said there's ghosts! Some geezer drowned in a well there.'

Gary found himself admiring the lush grounds and imagining posh people strolling around with parasols and whatnots. He wondered what the quickie guide would have entailed, for in a second they were on a main road again, albeit a narrow one, and fields were rushing past him.

Away from the coast the sharp breeze left his eyes, and he started to admire the neat fields when she briefly mentioned something about Kingsgate and Botany Bay, and then they were climbing uphill, and there was the coast again and a pub called the Captain Digby. The beach below looked very alluring to Gary, the thought of a wander along its sands tempting.

'More than one poor soul died there,' she said, 'car plunged right through the railings. My mate's dog fell over there once, too,' she added, 'bounced, shook his head and run off in the water!'

She roared off past Kingsgate Castle, the wind stealing her words, even through the mic.

'I hate the way they leave flowers on railings now, don't

you?'

The scooter held left and sped along an even narrower road, and Gary spied golfers out the corner of his eye, a panorama of green, flags and sandpits. Ahead of him a lighthouse shone its stark whiteness against a blue sky, a skirt of cabbages around its feet. On his left another beach, Joss Bay: this one in sharp contrast to Margate, just the one shop displaying rubber rings and buckets and spades, with white sand sparkling through the gap. To his delight she turned into the cliff-top car park, edged with cabbages going to seed, and paused there for him to admire the scenery.

'Grab an ice cream if you want one,' she said.

She waited whilst he did so, her face breaking into a smile as he wandered back to the scooter carrying two 99s.

'That's good of you, mate, she said, 'they're not real dairy either, so that's fine for me.'

'Nice bay this,' Gary said, watching the surfers.

They ate their ice creams, Gary standing, she sitting. Spotting the loo, he made for it, remembering he'd not been on the train, and on his way back wondered what she did when nature called. But he couldn't voice that thought, bit of a gentleman, Gary; so off they went, up past the lighthouse and then a turn left through what looked to Gary like a well posh estate. Warnings, gated entrances, pretend Tudor, the lot.

'Why're we here?'

'Thirty Nine Steps,' she answered. They came to the end of the road and there was the coast again, and she turned right, passing all the more splendiferous houses staring out to sea and paused at a grassy verge. She indicated an iron gate rusted into an old wall. Gary walked across and rattled it. It was padlocked, but through the railings he could see a row of concrete steps descending darkly downwards to what he guessed was the beach. He shrugged and climbed back on, shaking his head.

'Seen the film?' she asked.

'Naw.'

'Me neither,' she said, 'something to do with Germans, I think.'

She had to slow up riding into Broadstairs. They moved as slow as carthorses through the narrow street, Gary's bum warm from the engine and the sun. Cars nosed their way out of the car park; others cruised down Harbour Street. She pointed out the tiny cinema, (she seemed to have a thing for small places), and rode through the York Gate which, she quipped, was built for fishermen and animals, not bloody cars. There was an old wooden fishermen's building looking as if it was about to fall over any second, (she pointed out where Old George used to sit mending his nets), and an attractive pier with wooden seating and a café, and kids diving off the harbour wall. From the car park she pointed out the various beaches, Viking and Stone Bay, which, she said, joined up back the way they came, well worth the walk, at low tide of course. One or two fishing boats were hauled up on the beach, amid the sound of sandy children laughing and gulls screeching. She looked longingly at the sea.

'My family spend a lot of time out there,' she said.

'We've pencilled you in for lunch in Ramsgate,' she said, as they climbed back up through the York Gate and through the town, which to Gary's eyes, looked particularly well stocked with places to eat. He would have liked to stop there. Delis, Italians, Indians, Chinese as well as those boutique eateries … he'd have had a job choosing.

The town centre was tight and busy; buses seemed to hold up everything; they were forced to stop on more than one occasion. Gary didn't mind one bit when his guide increased her speed and wove her way through. Drivers blew their horns, and one or two raised their fists. He heard her laugh then, and found himself doing that too. What the hell?! In less than five minutes they were through Broadstairs and speeding along the Ramsgate Road. If Gary thought they were headed for another coastal tour he was wrong.

She slowed down and pointed out the changes to the road layout by an old pub called The Brown Jug; once famous, she said, for live poetry and French petanque. She pointed a group of large mock-Tudor houses crammed together.

'Used to be a lovely big bungalow there, white and blue Spanish hacienda type thing, garden always full of flowers. Can't credit it, can ya?'

' 'ouses, 'ouses, 'ouses' … you ever hear that song by The Imagined Village? Top band, worth checking out. On your right used to be rough land, the coaches used to park there, as many as a dozen on a Friday bringing hundreds of people to the market, and the Greyhound Racing. Naw, none 'o that ain't there no more. No Ramsgate Market, no Greyhound Racing. Place used to be packed, I tell ya. From summer to Christmas and summer again. But there ya go, things change don't they? That Poundland's stolen their thunder if you ask me.'

'Nice garden centre, though,' Gary offered.

He heard her sigh over the mic.

She turned off the road, and Gary was surprised to see a sign for Ramsgate Cemetery. She paused at the gate, indicated the tree-shaded driveway.

'This is an optional extra,' she said. 'No better way to know a place than find out who lived there.'

She noted Gary's hesitation.

'No? Don't worry; it's not for everyone. Rossetti's in Birchington anyway.'

She rode up and down various streets, pointing out the sites of murders and explosions, a hidden synagogue, buildings that used to be art centres, and the old Hovis flour mill. She got angry then, saying something about monstrosities and brownfield sites, and then they were heading uphill, and before he knew it there was the sea again. Gary felt his spirits lift. He'd seen pictures of the marina, but this was something special. The boats bobbed with joyous abandon on their musical moorings. Their approach led them down an almost hairpin bend along which she indicated a waterfall, which, she said, he was lucky to see working and was where she'd had her first shag. At the bottom of the hill she steered the scooter right through the bollards on the prom and turned the engine off.

'Lunch,' she said. She indicated the pub across the road, The Royal, and said there'd be a Seafarer's Special waiting for him, and to meet her back here in thirty minutes. Then she stood up, unplugged her earpiece, raised her arms, and dived gracefully into the marina.

Gary was caught short. With surprise that is. He looked around but no one was taking any notice. People were doing what they do, walking, pausing, looking at the sea, eating ice creams. Kids whined. A drunk leaned into Gary and asked if he could spare a fiver. Below him, in water streaked with oil and littered with beer cans and mouldy chips which the seagulls ignored, preferring to soar overhead and dive down on unsuspecting chip bags, he saw his guide frolicking and diving with what he could only describe as abandoned pleasure. She disappeared under the yachts only to come up the other side, basking belly-up on the water. She saw him watching and made several pointing gestures to her wrist. It dawned on Gary she was reminding him of the time.

He dragged his eyes away from her and crossed the road where, as she'd said, lunch was waiting. He ate it on one of their special window seats, open to the sea. A pint came with his Seafarer's Special, which, as he thought, was fish and chips, and wondered idly if the catch was local. He was never very good at history, but he did know fishermen had an industry once. He couldn't tell you if he was eating cod or coley.

By the time he'd lunched and paid another visit to the loo, thirty minutes was up. He could see her waiting across the road.

The drunk was leaning in the doorway. 'All right, mate?' He had startling eyes, deep azure. 'You one o' them developer people? I used to have an house once, I did,' he offered. 'Went round the world on one of *those* as well.' He indicated the yachts. 'You never know, boyo, do you?'

Gary sidestepped him and crossed by the lights. She was sitting on the scooter, engine running, hair wet and decorated with a ring pull from a can. She'd changed her top for a yellow T-shirt. Her arms were almost luminous.

She nodded. 'Good lunch?'

He nodded too, feeling alive and yet oddly non-conversational. She drove along the seafront, pointing out the continuing development on the site that had once held amusements, including a helter-skelter and a waltzer. She drove up the hill, pointing out where the disco Nero's used to be, and the open-air swimming pool. Now that, she told him, had been a sight to behold. Punters in all their swimming things posing and lounging on the diving boards, the sea beyond. The first infinity pool. Now, under all that debris and concrete, the old dressing rooms were still intact, and she could tell him a thing or two about malarkeys there!

She left him with an image of a Ramsgate packed with visitors from pleasure ships, stage coaches and horses, Victorian travellers pouring out amid the steam trains, breathing in the sea air they thought good for their health. She pointed out the walled-in entrances to tunnels, again hinting at a childhood layered with an intimate memory that seemed strangely timeless, and he wondered again at the state of her fingernails.

His bum had got quite comfy on the seat, and when she sped up again, doubling back along the Plains of Waterloo, past the waterfall and the marina, her commentary fed him bits and pieces of information: the Sailors' Mission below, the Smack Boys' home, the ferry port. She threw other names past him, like Pugin, but confessed to forgetting where he fitted in.

'Don't ask me nothing 'bout dates,' she said, 'I'm shit at dates. Nelson, wars, Edward Heath, fires, bombs, the synagogue, the first Chinese. I can't tell you all that. What I can show you is layers, layers and layers of lives lived, people with dreams and hard times like you and me. If I could, I'd show you the grave of the unknown African.'

'Unknown African? What unknown African?'

'There's unknown soldiers everywhere, ain't there? And monuments. Well, there's unknown Africans too, innit? What I can do is introduce you to someone. But first I'll run by Waitrose.'

She turned right down by the main car park, and rode up Queen Street.

'Place was boarded up for yonks before they built this,' she said. 'Can't remember what was there before. You can't, can ya? Remember everything?'

There was a nice little café opposite Waitrose.

'Used to be public toilets, that!' she volunteered.

She roared up the hill, pointing out the grammar school, the renovated library and slowed down past Ellington Park. 'How are you with scary stories?' she asked.

'Why?'

She laughed. 'Don't let me put you off; there's more to this lovely park than you see! Grisly murder, tunnels! Now that's a night out for you! Join the secret tunnel explorers' society!' The parakeets were screaming louder than her engine as they roared past.

Then she was riding through St Lawrence. 'One of the original parts of Ramsgate, this," she said, 'a village back then; imagine!' She turned into a narrow side street with terrace houses, and pulled up outside an iron gate smothered with dog roses. She pressed the horn. After a short while the door opened, and a small woman with a stoop and grey curly hair stood there. She was wearing a frock in a print of flamingos.

She smiled up at them.

'Oh, hello ducks! How're you today?'

'Fine, fine, Beatrice. This is Gary. Knows nothing.'

'Hello young man, you got a nice day fer it, intcha! Enjoy your lunch?'

Gary nodded, not sure what to say.

'Oh well, you never know what you're eating today, ducks. Time was you knew a flounder when you saw one. Whelks and mussels, eels.'

'We haven't got long, Bee, darling...'

'Sorry, ducks! Time getting on, is it? Well, Gary love, I've got a mobile now, yes, my daughter Millie made sure I've got one, just in case, she says, for emergencies...'

'Bee...'

"Yes I know, ducks, I ramble, but it's so important for these young people to imagine a time when you had to wait for news, you know ... when letters took days, and when a fishing boat was lost, oh dear, the waiting ... but he was my great grandfather, you see, and all we knew was, he was an African, and nobody knew how he got here, no; whether he came as a slave or not. But he was free then, see, yes a working black man, used to collect the glasses for the Watermen's Arms, the Northern Belle now. Have you taken him there yet, ducks? No? Oh well, that's where he heard all the stories, see, and Lord the commotion when he took up with our Maisie! Well, that's it, dearie, I don't know where they buried him, they never wrote his name or anything, see. But I've got his curly hair, see!"

She laughed and patted her hair, and ended by telling them both to take care on that dangerous vehicle, and how it was a pleasure, Gary, come back again.

Gary's head was spinning. He hadn't expected that encounter. His eyes were taking in the changing scenery, coming out of small streets, meeting new roads, petrol stations, fields, the sea offshore, circling. She headed down through Cliffsend where a Viking Ship sat tethered to the ground against a backdrop of sea and mudflats she swore used to harbour hovercrafts, but were only inhabited now by dippers; then cut through the villages, Minster with its Abbey settled like it had been there forever, Manston, where apart from a solitary cargo plane, the airport sat lonely, oddly post-war, with high fences and old hulks rusting on the edge of the tarmac.

His guide shook her head when he asked about that, seeing in his mind's eye the potential for foreign travel, flights straight to Majorca, Madeira, Crete. He saw traffic the other way as well, noisy Italians climbing down the airplane steps and breathing in the welcome sight of green fields and sea in the distance and Americans coming for the golf. But they rode past, with a little interlude, as she called it, through Acol, pointing out Quex Park, and hinting he might like to visit there sometime, perhaps when they had Jessie J and Plan B back again. They got rained off, she explained, last year. He might like to check out the museum itself, full of bones and treasures acquired from a colonial world of white explorers, if he was into that sort of thing. 'Friend of mine from the Caribbean had a literature festival there once,' she added, 'in a tipi. Powell-Cotton strolled round, watching them put it up. He looked a bit mystified.'

They were coming into Birchington, and as she had

said, Rossetti was on the agenda. They pulled into the car park behind the church, and she showed him where to go, pulling out a packet of fags from the top-box. The smell of the lit cigarette followed him as he walked through the churchyard, wandering aimlessly along the paths until he found what he was told to look for, right by the church door.

He stood for a while and stared down at it, wondering why he was doing so at all. Who the flipping heck was Rossetti anyway? And why Birchington? At his feet lay the remains of some artist, who nevertheless was just bones, what they'd all become. His mind ran on the unknown African then, and wondered about the possibility of his bones interred in this very graveyard. Then he thought further, of what exactly they all stood for, including him, and what he would leave of himself when he died.

Bloody hell. He was getting morbid. He made his way back to the scooter where his tourist guide was lounging, head down, texting. 'All right, Gary? Yeah, I know; dunno why they include this on the itinerary. They're thinking of doing Margate too, some guy called Sanger and some girls called the Tennyson sisters – they sound sort of musical to me.'

They roared back into Margate, and she drove up the ramp of the NCP car park. The Argyle House tower block roared up in front of them, the sea beyond, and the remnants of the funfair on their right. Beyond, a shine of new flats.

'Right, now you need to use your imagination,' she said. 'I ain't even gonna go into the whole story of glory days, of punters pouring off boats, and then trains and motorbikes on a Bank Holiday, to climb in them bathing machines or visit The Hall by the Sea or ride on Ferris wheels and waltzers, or what the bloody hell they're going to do wi' it now. This is just a pit stop to think about the word itself: Dreamland. Dreams. We all have them. The people who built *that* monstrosity had them. There's more than one life fell out that window! Everyone who stops to look at that muddy sea has them; even them in them old paintings of the Lah-di-das coming in off the hoys, holding their petticoats and their monocles high. Even now the powers that be are discussing whether or not to plonk another Tesco right here on the very spot. I ain't taken you everywhere, you'll need a week for that. I ain't taking you to the Shell Grotto either, that ain't on my list. You can go there yourself and wonder who the bugger was who planted all them shells. If he was an alien or some piss artist, don't really matter; what's left is left. But what we have to remember is what we step over when we start planting our dreams.

Over there, by the train line is where they had them animal cages. You know 'bout that? Wild animals. Elephants and tigers and lions. Was somebody's dream to bring them here, imprison them. Use them for *entertainment*. To offer the public dreams, as they had the right to expect them. I guess you can tell I ain't no poet, but in that bus shelter over there by the Nayland Rock (what used to be a well-posh hotel, horses and carriages and all) a poet called Eliot wrote something 'bout "nothing connecting nothing". Anyway, Gary, this is the final stop, and on behalf of the Alternative Tourist Committee, we hope you enjoyed your trip. Please tell your friends. Oh, and I've got a form for you to fill in, for the funding you know. Now let's get you back to the station.'

The scooter roared into the car park. Gary mumbled his thanks, and climbed down.

On his way into the station he heard her voice: 'Arlene! Oi, Arlene!'

Butterflies

Suraya slipped into the toilets by Peacocks. There wasn't a proper mirror there, only those ones made of steel where your face ghosted out at you. She pushed one of the doors open and squeezed in with her schoolbag. She sat down on the closed lid, reached in amongst her books for her make-up bag. There was a mirror inside the lid, and she squinted in the poor light as she applied foundation, smoothing her fingers across her skin, careful not to form streaks. Eye-shadow, silver and blue, highlighter, then mascara, a new one, purchased surreptitiously as it all was, on a Saturday afternoon at Superdrug with her cousin Amina. They'd both tried out false eyelashes, practising on each other in Amina's flat. Auntie was more lenient, more open to these things. 'Girls is girls,' she'd say, laughing, and would often tell Suraya's brother, Ahmed, to lighten up and get real. Ahmed, flexing his shoulders in his new leather jacket, was not to be trifled with. But they all decided none of them needed false eyelashes, all their lashes were long, luscious, curled like Bollywood film stars.

After the lipgloss, she held the mirror away. Now she looked normal. She wondered what her brother would say if he saw her like this. When she left the flat they shared in Cliftonville, she wore her headscarf and no make-up. She adjusted the front of her hair, pulling wisps out of the front to fall over her eyes like that girl Diane did. Not as if she liked her or anything, but she was one of those who stormed through the corridors with her gang in tow, always loud and laughing. Suraya zipped up her make-up bag, and was about to get up when she heard voices and the sound of doors banging.

'Hang on, Fabes, I really need a piss.'

'Well hurry up, I've got something to sort out with Adam before school. He's doing my head in, he is.'

'What's going on wiv you two? I thought you was sweet?'

'I'll tell you lata, I seen one 'o them pikey girls come in 'ere, probably earwigging us.'

'Yeah? Who?'

'Don't ask me, they all look the same to me.'

Suraya felt her face grow hot. She stood frozen, her hand on the latch. She heard the sound of the toilet being flushed, and the door being banged open. She heard whispering and laughter, then silence.

She took a breath and slid the bolt. Her face swum before her.

The Year 9 English boys were kicking each others' knees in the corridor. Playing war games. One held his mobile phone up high, recording the expressions of pain.

'Oh man! You wouldn't last five minutes! Five minutes of torture and you'll fess up everything!'

'Yeah, betray your country! Div!'

'Tosser!'

'I'll never be a fighter, man! I'm a lover not a fighter!'

'That ain't wot Diane said 'bout you man! Sez you couldn't even get it up!'

'YEAR 9! WHAT's going on here!'

Mr Eliot was marching up the corridor, his voice preceding him like a boomerang.

'Line up, you lot! Didn't you hear the bell? Clarkson, give me that phone right now!'

Suraya took her chance and slipped through the gang, taking her place in the line next door, where Year 8 were being shouted at to turn off their phones, stop yakking and find their seats immediately.

They always sat in the same places: Nesta, Fatima, Suraya, Amina in the second row; the two boys from Lithuania by the end wall; the Polish girls behind them. The Margate boys right at the back where they rocked their chairs incessantly against the wall. The boys from London were placed in the front by the tutor, but always ended up at the back, chairs turned round, sharing jokes and mobile uploads under the table. Last week a Somali boy had joined the class, a small, bird-boned boy who had yet to say a word and whose eyes were consistently staring out the window.

The interpreter, Avril, came into the class, smiling. Suraya liked her, she was calm and pretty, and knew how to get round the boys, although Suraya still could not understand why so much bad behaviour went unpunished. It was one of the many things Suraya did not understand.

There were more mysterious things than language. She could easily translate words, could find out at a click what a word meant. But a word didn't always mean what you thought. Think of 'Gypsy'. Try as she might Suraya couldn't think of that word without the image of the wall that had split her hometown right down the middle. That's not what the dictionary offered. She looked out of the classroom window, over the rooftops of the grey brick buildings. A solitary seagull stood on a chimney, his white body fat against a dull sky.

The wall had been grey. It had risen up quickly, after months of rumours, running alongside the trainline, and splitting the village from the main shops and the school. For Suraya and the children it was a strange thing, finding you could no longer move freely around a place you thought was home. Even the woods had become out of bounds, not surprising, there were still wild boar to be found, prime meat in the hard times, and songbirds, tiny fluttering bodies trapped in nets. Her mother would tell them of times she remembered, when the apartments they lived in were new, when the lift worked, when the Communists ruled. Everyone had jobs then too, her mother would say, watching her father pull on his pipe as he leaned on the frayed elbows of his jumper on the balcony. Suraya tried to imagine her father going off to work each day. He had grown even more silent after the wall was built. He had ceased to comment even when her mother had come in after a day of seeking laundry work, any kind of work, by knocking on doors the other side of the wall, covered in slush and urine.

Suraya tried to stop thinking of home, had blocked out events leading from these general impressions to the night when they were bundled, her and her brother, into the back of a van.

There was a stranger in the classroom, a new teacher. Suraya heard their tutor introduce her, say something about poetry. Watched her step forward wearing jeans and a top crowded with butterflies. The boys in the back row were momentarily quiet, waiting to see what treat they had in store, what diversion in the day. Suraya heard the tutor ask the class to be respectful, and went out of the room. The new teacher opened a book and began to read, something about a child learning to walk. The words bounced over her. All she could see were the butterflies rising en masse at the edge of the dark woods.

The boys were talking amongst themselves. The teacher stopped reading and asked them to be quiet, as others wanted to listen. Avril too, sitting amongst them, turned and used her soft voice saying please be respectful. The new teacher's voice was not as bold as it was the first time. The door opened and Sharmila entered. She walked to the back of the class and stood against the wall, her coat and bag clutched close. The new teacher asked her to find a seat. There was an empty seat near to the two English girls who had been in the toilets this morning; they sat with their heads together whispering. Sharmila ignored the teacher and stared at the floor.

The teacher tried to read from the book again. Bursts of laughter broke from the Margate boys. They were watching a YouTube video under the desk. Suraya and the girls either side of her looked at each other and shrugged. Apart from herself and Amina, they all spoke different mother tongues; were learning to speak to each other in this new tongue, this raw brash language, which was three different languages: the one Avril was teaching them to speak, the one they heard in the street, *fucking refugee, terrorist, Muslim bitch, dirty pikey,* and the one they heard on telly on *Hollyoaks* and *Eastenders* where the girls all looked wicked with their hair and eyes. Amina passed her a chewing gum under the desk.

Her father had read her a poem once. He had reached up to the top of the wardrobe and pulled out *A Child's Treasury of Poems,* an English book he had acquired from somewhere, and had read her 'The Owl and the Pussycat', in slow stumbling English. Suraya remembered some of the words : "the owl and the pussycat went to sea in a beautiful pea green boat…"

The boat they had boarded after weeks of driving in the back of vans, lorries, and at one time, an old ambulance, had not been beautiful or pea green. It had been a large rumbling ferry with four cargo decks, a corner of which Suraya, Ahmed and four other people had eventually been discovered, amongst crates of olives.

One of the English girls, Phoebe/Fabes raised her hand. 'Miss! Miss!'

The new teacher raised her head from the book. She looked eager to reply. 'Yes?'

Fabes inclined her head in the direction of Sharmila. 'She's crying, Miss.'

'What?'

The teacher looked unnerved. She put down the book, walked to the back of the class, and spoke softly to Sharmila. Sharmila ignored her. Her tears fell, silently, down her plump cheeks. Suraya could see her mascara beginning to run. The new teacher looked round helplessly. Avril pushed her chair back and went to join them. She was asking if Sharmila didn't feel well, if she'd like to sit in the office for a while. She moved closer to Sharmila then stopped. Suraya heard her say to the new teacher, 'It's all right, she's just a bit upset, you carry on'.

Suraya watched the new teacher's faltering steps as she spotted the mobile phone gang, eyes on their laps. The big boy who leaned back against the wall said something with bad words in, and Suraya felt the new teacher recoil.

'Isn't that poetry, Miss? It's poetry innit, Miss!'

The butterflies on her top danced as she moved back to the front of the class. She started to write on the board then, ideas for a poem. Asked for words to start, any word. The big boy shouted 'Oik', Fabes shrugged and said 'Love', Amina giggled, put up her hand and offered 'Girl Power'. They were asked to find their own words then, and write a poem, and after five minutes the new teacher started to walk round the glass looking at all the empty pages, everyone shrugging and saying they didn't know what to write, and Fabes said loudly how long did they have to do this shit for. When the new teacher came to Suraya, Suraya's chest was hammering inside her, bang bang bang bang bang bang, and she used the first word that came into her head, 'butterflies', and the teacher smiled, raising the material on her top so Suraya could see the butterflies printed there as wild and free as the ones that had risen up when Suraya's mother had gone into the woods searching for her father, beating back the ferns by the river with a stick, her neighbours and Ahmed and Suraya in a line, spread out, calling her father's name, disturbing the heron, and then a sudden burst of colour lifted from the reeds, their wings turquoise and diaphanous, filigree-thin and transparent, through which the dark shape of her father's body appeared angled like a ladder against a tree.

The words drowned in her throat, she turned to look out of the window.

The seagull was still standing there. As she watched, two of the green birds that lived in the park dropped down on the windowsill. The gaze of the Somali boy moved from one to another. Suraya saw him twitch sometimes when there was a sudden noise, like a chair falling, or one of the boys throwing something loud against the wall.

Let's Dance

ndra squealed to a stop outside the Winter Gardens. She jumped out in a flurry and flicked the child locks open, freeing two tortoises and a witch's cat. The tortoises had been fighting in the back, and as a result one had his carapace around his neck and the other had lost a foot. Indra was irate; the foot in particular had taken a long time to create, with strips of real leather with glue *and* stitches. She doubted if she could make it look as perfect again.

Around her, Nissans and Audis were nose to tail. A BMW had its front wheels on the pavement. Across the road the fat mum with the ugly twins was waiting to cross.

Indra shooed her tribe down the steps, the wind whistling and cutting as usual, and headed for the swing doors. There was a choir of meerkats pressed up against the inside door; the tail of one appeared to have been trodden on, and a pair of Minnie Mouse knickers was in full view. Tears had erupted, she guessed not only due to the effect of the impropriety but by the packed foyer inhabited by a menagerie that included seahorses, crabs, and a tiger. Dotted amongst them were the tinies in frothy tutus.

A jolt in the back told Indra they were backing up on the steps too, a quick look behind her into the amber eyes of what appeared to be a bear, identified a huddle of marmosets and a chimpanzee. For a minute she felt quite giddy, she'd never really liked zoos or circuses, and she was beginning to feel she was in one. At least it wasn't hot, the April offering from the Channel ushered a crisp breeze through the side doors.

She caught sight of the marmosets' mother and exchanged a mutual smile.

Over a collection of animated heads, comments flew back and forth. What on earth were they letting themselves in for? Didn't they have enough last year? Plus there was the parking, they should have known it would not be as simple as a drop and run. Blinking traffic wardens. Typical Thanet.

As if on cue, a short dumpy figure, weighed down with Aldi carrier bags and a snorkel was pushing her way down through the gathering. She was well acquainted with all the animals, and kept up a running commentary as she descended

'Jason you look fabulous o my goodness Liam you are well scary and Sammy wow you look amazing did Mummy do that? My my sorry oops didn't knock your head off did I Tilly? O clever mummies I am so sorry guess who's late? What am I like – so sorry – oh thanks – I'll just squeeze through…'

Behind her, a tall skinny husband followed, lifting a cardboard box overhead. He only said things like 'Mind out, watch your heads,' so not many took notice, pushing forward after the lure of the Aldi carrier bag that offered them entrance to the hall at last.

Indra watched the figures in the foyer part like the proverbial waters, seahorses, crabs, carrier bags, snorkel and cardboard box breaking through the thin-lipped demeanour of the security person who lifted the chain across the entrance to the stairs, allowing the tumble downwards of hooves, claws, tails and paws.

'Thank Christ for that,' one of the mums said, 'out here much longer we'll be going in with the audience!'

'We *are* the audience aren't we?'

'You'd be surprised how many nans and granddads there are! Was standing room only last time. At least being helpers we can grab the front seats!'

In less than ten minutes the front three rows of the hall were covered with coats, handbags and lunch boxes. They'd been warned to bring snacks as there was no catering not till later. Packets of Mars bars, Wotsits, Maltesers and Pringles appeared, and wrappers and squashed juice cartons begun to decorate the upholstery.

The Dance School owner and hubby were ensconced in dialogue with at least ten people all at the same time. There was The List to be dug out and adhered to, the music to be sorted, the lighting man to be brought up to date with the latest changes, the trophies to be displayed on top of the piano. There were the helpers to be assigned their charges, in order of dance class, and last but not least, the mummies to be seen to. To make things perfectly clear, she climbed the stairs of the stage and clapped her hands, a feat that only had resonance when someone to do with the theatre helpfully plugged the mic in, and she relinquished a cough and a 'one-two, one-two, testing'. The mummies were straightaway told they were welcome to stay but please, please make sure that they were in full possession of their tickets, as this show just could not happen, could not in the slightest cover the full cost of the production without everyone's contribution. Indra and several of the mummies looked at each other and rolled their eyes. They mouthed the words *costumes* and *contribution*.

'I'll have to go and move the car,' Indra said, 'you guys sit here and don't wander off.' She made her way through the aisle of sleeping seats rapidly being awakened, backs lifted, and bodies taking possession, and out into the corridor. A flock of tall ballerinas were floating about in the foyer.

'Oh my God, is it true there's another performance going on here as well as ours?'

There were gasps of consternation.

'And OMG like they've got the best hall!'

'How on earth was that allowed to happen? No wonder Mummy couldn't find anywhere to park!'

'I know, isn't it just awful! Crikey do you think anyone's going to come to our show?'

A burst of laughter brushed the plastic fronds of a potted palm.

'Oh you pillock, Serena! It's our *Awards* night for Chrissake! Thelma Laycock herself is coming from the NDPA! Do you really think there is going to be any competition from that little dance and drama thingy … what are they called?'

'The Silver Spangles.' Ballerina laughter tinkled into the air again.

Indra caught sight of the thin-lipped attendant, who had crossed to the other stairs and had lifted the golden chain.

'Will you girls please move along,' she heard her say.

Indra's car keys jangled from her fingers as she made for the outer door. Dotted amongst the gelled heads of smoothly made-up children skipping their way down the stairs, the bushy tail of a squirrel and a kangaroo's hand-knitted pouch flitted.

She started her car and headed along the road looking for somewhere to park. On her left the Channel growled its surly way, a cargo ship un-moving on the horizon.

The stuck-up girls were right, there was nowhere to

park. Except Lidl. She guessed she could park in Lidl. She cruised in and found a spot. Guilt sent her inside to purchase a six pack of apple juice. It was a bit of a walk back, but what the hell.

She'd only been here two years. When you first come to a place you don't really know what to expect. 'You lucky things, going to live by the sea!' their friends had said.

And of course she was lucky. Not least because of the house. What with the money they got for their house in Stoke Newington, they'd been able to buy a large four-bedroom detached house in Palm Bay. At least it wasn't Cliftonville. At least they didn't make *that* mistake, thanks to the estate agent. She could so easily have been misled. And she was more than happy with the school, all the kids were happy. And when she saw the advert for the Silver Spangles, even Dennis was happy to go. She guessed there would come a time when he would realise the boys thinned out, that dancing was for girls and sissy for boys. She knew it would be no point arguing the unarguable, quoting from Mikhail Baryshnikov's documentary about the manly strength boy ballet dancers needed to lift girls. Now it was enough they were thrilled they were in the show too.

She crossed the road and headed back to the Winter Gardens. Cars were still dropping children off, some stood outside the theatre in small groups waiting for friends. She had been here before, she and Bobby had come to an eighties night with their neighbours hoping to let their hair down and have a laugh. Way to make friends too.

She liked to dance. Too much perhaps. She was dancing when she met Bobby, some club out in Harrow somewhere, she and her girlfriends going for it to soul music. But even before that, in front of the telly, copying Madonna. She'd begged and begged to go to ballet, street dance, anything, but no.

'You're having a laugh, aintcha, hon?' Her mum, out

cleaning all day and glued to the TV at night, had no truck with any of that kind of thing.

'You jest work hard and get a good job, Indra,' she used to say. 'Don't want you struggling like me. Bad enough you look so much like *him*.' And she'd look at the picture of Indra's dad, a boy called Haroun who had come to study in London and had made her pregnant before returning to some small country the other side of the world.

And so she had studied and worked hard; meeting Bobby was a plus, and here they were making their way, a new life by the sea. She didn't want to think it was the wrong way.

Something sent her down the stairs to the other dance performance in the Queen Elizabeth Hall. There were two women standing at the entrance, sorting tickets and money out on a table. Photographs of ballet dancers in various poses adorned a screen behind them. The name of the school was prominent and elegant on the posters, The Tileda Foster School of Dance. The women looked up and smiled.

'Hello, have you come to drop off or help?' They looked behind her for an invisible child.

'I ... I just wondered if I could have a peek – are they rehearsing?'

One of the women frowned. 'Have you got a child at the school?'

'Noo ... no, well, I have got a child, three in fact, I was thinking of...'

Understanding lit the woman's face. 'Oh! You want a peek, see what the show's like!' She smiled. 'Well, really you should buy a ticket, but it doesn't start for ages yet, and they are just doing a run through of ... let me see...' she flicked through the glossy brochure, 'Ah yes, it's Melanie and Sophia's show dance *Symphony for Martha Graham* ... I don't see any harm you slipping in and having a quick peek. If you're impressed I'm sure Mrs T would love you to have a look round the school.'

'Thank you!' She pushed the door open and entered the hall. For a moment she experienced a sense of déjà vu. She could have been standing in the other hall, the seats at the front were covered in coats and bags, and packets of crisps and cans of Coke flitted in and out of her view. But there was silence. Two girls commanded the stage, enacting what she understood to be contemporary dance. Their movements were fluid, with each phrase smoothly linked into another. She could see ballet training in their movements, the elongation of a limb, the grace in which they carried their heads. But she could also see a narrative, a fight with the body to dismiss its limitations and form shapes that didn't seem natural. They ended the dance sitting on the floor, back to back, heads arched upwards to the ceiling. She caught her breath, caught in a moment she couldn't define.

'They're lovely aren't they?' One of the women from the door had come up behind her. 'Headed for the Royal Ballet School, those two.'

'Thank you for letting me have a look,' Indra said.

'Hope to see you again; here, take a programme.'

Her steps up the stairway were light. They carried her along, past the thin-lipped woman, across the foyer where an audience was now beginning to queue and then downwards again, towards the other hall. Two of the mums were busy setting up a table by the entrance. She paused and rummaged in her bag for her ticket, leaving Bobby's in their care. She took a breath and re-entered the hall, feeling like a sailor pulling in to port, or an explorer. The only thing was, she didn't have a compass.

Homes Under the Hammer

Well, I can't say I understand too rightly exactly what you want. I don't know nuttin 'bout art. And, fer the record, you ain't using my real name.

So you want me tell you what it's like to grow up in Ramsgate? You talking to people in Margate and Broadstairs, too? Where you want me to start?

I suppose I can start by talking 'bout this house. Council pass over the tenancy when me mam went. She worked at Hornby all 'er life, and me dad on the railway. At least till his back went. She used to make jokes about first him and then her keeping us kids on track.

Lot of these were bought private, but my folks never believe in that shit. 'Steal 'ouses meant fer the poor?' me Dad used to say.

Not everyone think like that. When that thing 'bout equity hit the news, some people start get big ideas. Some even used to go round looking at 'ouses just fer the fun of it.

We called them the house groupies. They started off by pretending they wuz buyers by lying to the estate agents, then went out on a Sunday looking round people's houses. They wuz full of it, they wuz. Next thing they're on that TV show *Homes under the Hammer,* pretending they had money.

Marge and me lived next door to somebody jes like that when we wuz little. She was plain Susie then, but now she call herself Sheyvon, *Sheyvon!* She went up town and found some bloke from Gravesend to marry her, and somehow they managed to buy her mum's council house. That's how they got on the housing ladder. That's how they can put their hands up on *Homes Under the Hammer.*

To see her swanning on TV with her hair all done up talking about 'nice sized rooms' and 'great location' made me choke. There she was going on about a pissy house in Broadstairs, which was really Westwood for those in the know, and 'relocating to the area'. Jee-sus Christ, if it wasn't for the ASBO I'd be sorting her out good and proper like when we wuz at Conyngham. Course, even that's gone all uppity now, innit, first The Ramsgate School now it's an Academy, my dear.

There's one thing I can't stand is uppity people and liars. Every bleeding day I come across one or t'other. If it's not up the Council where some young un's lying 'bout her mum throwing her out 'cos she's preggers, it's some shop girl doing me outa change. See me, now, I ain't got no airs and graces. You tek me as you find me. I been on this estate since I was six, and I'm not budging until they tek me out in a pine box. Or mebbe not pine, mebbe one o' dem wicker ones in dem green funerals in a woods somewhere…

Dere's 'ardly any woods left now. When we wuz growing up there wuz woods. There wuz wild places all over. 'Tween 'ere and Broadstairs, 'tween there and Margate.

Me and Marge and me cousin Simon used to climb over the wall at Haine Hospital when we went nicking cabbages where Westwood Cross now is. Haine was full of trees and mad people and parrots. Not that I got anyfink against Westwood Cross. I ain't one o' dem protester types who waste their time demostartin' and putting themselves in the paper. Council want sell land, they gonna sell land. Jes like what gon happen to the airport gon happen to the airport; there's plenty of people had their eye on that land from day bloody one.

Don't get me wrong; I don't like nuttin betta than catch the bus and nose round them Westwood shops even if I ain't got a penny to me name. Darn sight nicer nosing round Marks in the warm than wander round the High Street like a ghost! You wouldn't believe how busy Margate town centre used to be! Me and me mates could spend all day in and out of Peacocks and Marks and Next and River Island and Burtons … all gone now. Fucking 'ell, I starting to sound like me nan!

Regeneration? I ain't so thick I can't 'preciate them arty farty shops, though fer the life o' me I can't see how anybody would pay three hundred quid fer an old chest like Nan kept her blankets in … anyway where was I? Oh yeah … so that Susie/Sheyvon, she gets herself an house on what she call the borders of Broadstairs … hee hee … she might be right, Broadstairs has borders for true! It call cabbage fields, it call money and nice house, but tell that to the lads and lasses pissed as coots on a Friday night! I think it call 'lowering the tone'.

Yeah, there wuz differences between the three, though you can't bloody see it now. That's what happens when they start cutting down trees. I remember me and Marge went on the open-top bus once, jes forra ride, like. Did the whole thing, from 'ere through Broadstairs, St Peter's, Kingsgate, looking down on who had swimming pools and train tracks running round them garden, right down the sea fronts, Margate, Minnis Bay and back. We had such a laugh, me and Marge! We must 'ave been 'bout ten. We wuz nose to butt with sightseers going 'Ooo Look!' And 'Awr, that's very nice, innit?' and, 'I promised my mother I would check out the old place for her' and 'Of course one can see how Turner was inspired'... everyone from Yankees to Cockneys to Frenchies. We wuz killing ourselves laughing we wuz! But you know, when I look back it weren't half nice really, seeing Thanet like a bird might, you know whatta mean? All them fields and the sea and everything. Though when you've had to nick the money for the bus fare and skive off school and hide yer school uniform in a plastic bag the whole bloody thing's just a laugh, innit?

Of course, them days there weren't no bloody law to stop you skiving off school, not like now when the bastards fining you a hundred pound if yer kids don't go. To tell you the truth, I think the teachers would have paid to have some of us stay away! You think I had control over my Trevor? You think I had control over a child what had ADHD, and that's how I lose these teeth here, see? But you don't want hear about that side o' things, do ya? You don't want hear about the fact that I have a letter sitting here telling me that after forty-five years living in this here 'ouse, having to care for me mum and dad and a useless wanker of an 'usband and then my Trev who, give him his due, still turns up when he needs help and who can refuse their own child a bed – after forty-five years it seem that I don't need a two bedroom 'ouse!?

It seem to me you want to hear me share my memories of candy floss and donkey rides and Pleasurama ... well, I had a shag round the back of the helter-skelter once with a fella called Dave if you're interested ...

And this art thing now, it have anything to do with that snooty cow I hear say the other day say 'God I really had to work hard to make things happen in this place?'!

You know, on second thoughts I don't think I want nobody to make no documentary 'bout me. Fact is, every blasted word you say somebody take it the wrong way. So if you don't mind, drink your tea and leave me be.

The Parakeet Café

Dilys got off the train at Margate and stood for a moment outside. There was building going on, work on the car park. She picked her way carefully past the taxis and paused at the busy roundabout. It was all so different, the roundabout, the traffic lights, the boards on her right where the funfair used to be. Ahead of her, however, the sea still shone; and the shelter sat as it always had, though not always as pristine. She'd sat there with Paul. On its left, the Nayland Rock Hotel. She couldn't remember anything about that, apart from seeing photos of horses and carriages in the drive in its heyday, well before her time. That was the sort of thing she did now, look at photos.

She made her way via the crossing and turned right, walking along the promenade. The palms in their large pots made her think of Torquay. In the distance, the Turner Gallery glinted like a schooner about to glide off into the sea. She'd seen it on TV.

'Mum, are you sure you don't want one of us to come with you?' her daughter Bella had asked again, when she dropped her at Reading.

'No, dear,' she'd said firmly. 'This is something I need to do on my own.'

She held her bag closely as she walked, aware of the package inside. It was light, lighter than she thought it would be.

She knew the Parakeet Café no longer existed, she hadn't lost her marbles just yet. There were a number of times in her life she had come close. When Cliff died, for instance, and when the girls left home. But she liked to think she was still compos mentis, as they say.

1965 it was; she'd met Paul here on holiday. 1965. She and her cousin, Felicity, just seventeen, brave enough to holiday on their own for the first time, had rented rooms in a boarding house in Cliftonville.

That first day they had headed straight for the beach, weighed down with freedom, weighed down with blue and white canvas bags, a packed lunch, rush mats and their own towels. 'You ain't tekking the towels from this establishment!' the landlady had warned. They'd called her the ogre, laughing behind her back. She looked like Ena Sharples. There were so many other warnings – breakfast prompt at 8, extra for sandwiches, no visitors, dinner at 6, doors locked at 11. At least she didn't mind them smoking. She herself had a cigarette permanently attached to her reddened lips as she brought them out plates of fried egg and bacon, which were surprisingly good. *Or maybe we didn't know what bad was,* Dilys thought now. Years of cooking her own food, and staying in nice hotels on holidays in Spain, Malta and Florida with Cliff and the girls had spoilt her. Back in 1965, all she wanted was to wolf down anything, tart herself up and take herself off out. 'I wonder if we were "fast"?' She giggled to herself, raising a look from a girl with a pushchair who had paused to light a cigarette.

Dilys caught a look at herself in the mirrored glass of the café opposite the Clock Tower. There she was, a little old woman, hair grey and tidy, short, dressed in a sensible jacket from Marks and Spencer's Spring Range.

'Crikey, you're a corker,' had been his first words.

She and Felicity had spent the morning lazing on the beach, and they had stirred themselves to go and get ice creams. He was tall with grey eyes, and hair like Roger Daltrey from The Who. His fingers had brushed hers as he passed her the change.

She had blushed, heat flushing her cheeks and neck, aware of her breasts in the yellow bikini, purchased for the holiday, and her hands automatically smoothed her chestnut hair which tumbled down her back. She and Felicity had giggled as they made their way across the sand.

That evening, they rushed their dinner, heading for quick showers whose thin trickles of water barely rinsed the sun oil and nuggets of sand off their skin and hair before it went cold. There was no use complaining. The ogre rubbed out a stub in the hallway ashtray and declared that the tank did not run to two showers a day, and there were twelve other guests staying in her establishment.

They'd found a local pub, downing Martinis and vodkas, making coy looks at boys whose attire ranged from smart to casual – suits, jeans, T-shirts, paisley shirts, medallions. There was a jukebox playing all the hits – the Dave Clark Five, Herman's Hermits, the Rolling Stones, the Beatles – and a floor for dancing, which they took to in their sling-backed shoes. No wonder they overslept that second morning, woken by a pounding on the door of the bedroom they shared, by a declaration that breakfast had been missed.

They were subdued as they went out later, making their

way along the busy Northdown Road, buzzing with cafés and shops bulging with pastries, furniture and linens, TV sets, china, clothes and shoes. The sea air blew their hangovers away, and they settled for a café primarily for its name, The Parakeet Café. It was simple and basic, tea and toast, scones, soup at lunch, chips. The proprietors were smiley and chatty, and young and old both sat at the tables deep in conversation or cupping steaming mugs of tea.

'Hello, Gorgeous.' He stood above her with a notepad in hand. The lad from the ice cream parlour. 'What can I get you for?'

Felicity giggled and ordered tea and toast for them. He didn't take his eyes off Dilys, though. She caught him watching her as he weaved between the tables, and then brought their orders.

As they rose to leave, he appeared and pulled their chairs out for them.

'Heading for the beach, ladies? See you later maybe?'

And so it had begun. Dilys had fallen like a meteor; at seventeen, love was instant. The boy with the grey eyes and the two jobs was Paul, and in his breaks from selling ice cream and waiting at tables, he played guitar and wrote songs. Breakfast in The Parakeet Café became the start to their day, and soon he was joining them on the beach in his off-shifts, nipping out for an hour or two to take them to Dreamland where he bought them candyfloss and licked Dilys's sticky fingers. Looking across now at the sad alley that had once led to the funfair, Dilys couldn't believe it was the same place that had been jam-packed with crowds queuing up for the rides, and where she had boarded a Ferris wheel for the first time, her heart dropping away at the town and the sea swirling below.

She flushed now as she remembered the first time she'd gone to his house. His mum was at work, and for two whole hours her body betrayed her as it opened to his mouth and fingers, his golden body, his energy. She remembered the guitar leaning against the wall, and when she asked him to play her something, the way he leaned his naked body across the bed and reached for it.

In the evening, he had taken her and Felicity down to Hades nightclub, where upturned beer barrels served as tables, and the sweet smell of foreign cigarettes curled from the corners of darkened rooms. They had danced to Pink Floyd there, Yes, and Santana.

She remembered telephoning her mother on Friday, pleading for another week, saying how much she and Felicity were enjoying the seaside and that it wouldn't cost much more. She didn't know why her mother relented; perhaps she recalled her own restricted wartime youth, or a husband snoring directly after dinner in his armchair. Her warnings to Dilys were coded, she must 'be careful' and 'don't do anything I wouldn't do'.

That second week, made cheaper by making an arrangement for lodging only, and conversely becoming more expensive by eating out at The Parakeet Café, became a week that Dilys would never forget, a week of sea and sand, bars and music, two pretty girls on the arms of a dashing young man and his friend Sam, and sex in snatched hours at Paul's house. Her heart and mind were making plans even as she knew it was just a holiday romance. 'Why should it be?' She asked Felicity. 'I can move, who cares about Secretarial College anyway?'

'Dils, we don't know what this place is like out of season! It could be a right heap! And what do you know about Paul really? I mean, he's 19, is he going to sell ice cream forever?'

'Don't be so mean, Fliss! He's going to be a musician!'

'Yeah, right! Going on tour with the Who, is he?'

'He's written a song for me!'

'Ha Ha! You poor girl, when we leave, there's bound to be other girls!'

She bit her lip then, not knowing how to describe the evening before, after they'd made love, when he'd sat cross-legged on the bed and started to strum a melody. She was still curled up in bed and giggled as he started to make up a song, rhyming 'girl' with 'curl' and getting cross when he couldn't find a rhyme for 'bikini'.

He came to the station to see them off, holding Dilys tight against him. She remembered the feel of his hair against her cheek, and the way he cupped her face in his hands. 'I will never forget you,' he had said.

He didn't.

At first they tried to work round the difficulties that stood in their way – jobs and college, distance. They spoke on the telephone, and tried to make plans, which never happened. Weeks turned into months, and then he got the break he had been waiting for, a tour of Europe with a band.

After that tour was another tour. He sent her postcards from countries as far apart as Australia and Canada, Berlin and Japan. Dilys couldn't reply; he never seemed to be in the same place long enough. She remembered the moment she saw him on Top of the Pops singing the song she had heard him strum in Margate, 'The Girl in the Yellow Bikini'. It made Number One, and she had got a phone call then, his voice rushed and jubilant saying that it was mad, it was all mad, they were off to Madrid the next day, and how much he wished they could have met up, how he owed the song to her. Some months later, he had sent Dilys the Gold Record. By that time she had met Cliff.

She had a special drawer for it all, the gold record, the postcards. Cliff, her husband by then, turned a blind eye, even that one time they went to see Paul, after the concert at the O2, the tickets arriving by courier, the car sent. The one meeting: in his dressing-room, his manager hovering, Cliff awkward behind; Dilys's heart had hammered like a pneumatic drill, looking for the grey-eyed boy behind the dark glasses. Over the years, the newspaper reports, his failed marriages, the custody suits; the boy from Margate who'd worked at The Parakeet Café and had made it big through the song about the mystery girl in the yellow bikini.

When the news came it wasn't a surprise to Dilys, all those years of hard living had come to an end. What did surprise her was his request, which she carried now like a bouquet.

She knew she would not go to Cliftonville, looking for the Parakeet Café. She knew it was no longer there.

She walked past the Turner Gallery to the Harbour Arms, rows of new small businesses set into the walls. Pictures and postcards, mugs decorated with Tracey Emin's scribbles. The Shell Ladies stood looking over the sea. They watched her as she opened her bag, take the small container out and shake it like confetti over the singing waves.

The Flight Path

Did they ask us? No. Are they building bridges, digging underground passages so we might cross safely? No. Are they lifting us carefully with chamois leather gloves for transportation to greener, uninterrupted fields? No. Naturally, the idea that anyone would bring themselves to their knees and collect each one of us clinging to blades of grass, burrows, hedgerows, old pipes or broken containers, a Roman humerus, a Neolithic anvil; is too much to hope for. We are used to tractor wheels and harvesters, just as we were used to the flat soles of shoes, and dogs nosing. Just as we were used to hooves and whistles, foxes panting, ploughs, swords, rain, blood, the rabbits on the runway, the hares, the engines screaming, the planes lifting off, landing. Who will remember these fields, made fertile with our blood and bones, harnessed by seasons? Here now, the diggers come.

At the Nayland Rock the Poet Watched the Sea

"On Margate Sands.
I can connect
Nothing with nothing
The broken finger-nails of dirty hands
My humble people who expect
Nothing."
T.S. Eliot, The Waste Land

Never mind the damned birds; they've left me the last word. 'I can connect nothing with nothing?' Did I write that? That year, 1921, they say I cracked with a broken heart, sent me to Margate, to recuperate. Stayed at a placed called called The Albemarle, in Cliftonville. No longer there of course.

So much no longer there. Why should it be? Read my damned poem; see what was no longer there in 1921.

Of all the places in all the world I have to end up in this one ... *wandering lonely as a cloud...*

La la.

Sometimes it pays to wander, digress. Poets do it admirably. But to close ... why should an American have the last word? Why not Silas, or Nick, or Clyde? Why not that old fella there, staring out to sea? Or that kid on the skateboard making himself a nuisance on the sidewalk? The palms are looking a bit jaded, crisp at the frond. They don't like the darned wind.

The old place has certainly changed. Those council offices now – best view in the darned place, I bet. Busy making plans for others, sitting in their offices looking down at us humble lot with our dirty fingernails, huh?

This sure is the place for contemplation. I watch them come, the gay ones, arms round each other, skipping along ... oh, dammit, that word's 'out' now, isn't it? Never mind, time passes so quickly, like these young mothers with their strollers, French fries, ice creams. Then there are the soldiers, weary-eyed, knapsacks; they don't wanna go back, no Sir. There's thunder too, lots of it, Harleys between their thighs roaring the heavens, shrugging their leather jackets off, giving the world the benefit of their tattoos. Go on guys, life is short! Oh and a little flurry of nuns, the kids trailing behind like ducklings, stealing a glance at these enticing sands! Off they go, stiff breeze before the Angelus. Latin next. And, dammit, here come the Krauts dropping their blasted bombs, ripping those streets I strode to smithereens. There's a woman lying face down on the pavement. I think the poor soul is a goner.

Through all these tales I've been listening, offered words now and then, phrases to make you pause. You may have not noticed; so many of you say poetry's not for me, but then you reach for it for when someone's died. Well, let me tell you, poetry was the first language, the first communicator. Ask those troubadours lilting their secret messages. Ask how they carried the news from Ghent to Aix. Ask Wilfred Owens. Ask the pigeons. Step through their poops on the pavement, but watch the way they're watching you, the rhythmiticky way they walk, uh huh, uh huh. And I guess you better ask those noisy parakeets too, looks like they're here to stay.

There's that sly Silas walking his walk to connive and sail. Who's to know he didn't get what he planned, his own house high on the cliff and a nice little business dealing in silks and tobacco? His descendants might be passing you right now in the streets, drenching you with rainwater from the wheels of a BMW, rich from the profits of dealing whatever it is they're imbibing now.

There's a girl on the beach now, gathering seaweed. She speaks to me sometimes, asking have I seen her mother? She carries a bronze cup in her hand, an eagle embossed. Those that sit beside me come and go; not all see me. There's a lad called Daniel, drives a yellow campervan, parks by the station and settles here with his girlfriend looking at the sea. She's in a wheelchair.

And here comes that guy called Clyde, and his son, always on his mobile. And the little girl Hilary, skipping beside her granddad, he's pointing out the Unknown Soldier, eyes out to sea. Her granddad can see me. So can Nick; not that *he* speaks, he's more the pensive type. He likes to come and watch those guys, the Red Arrows, when they do their thing. Well now, *that's* a sight to see, the beach packed to the gunnels, just like the '80s when the BBC did this thing … now what was it called now … a Road Trip … a Road … Show, yes that was it, disc jockeys right on this very beach here and all the girls screaming their pretty heads off.

It gets mighty busy in this shelter sometimes. Very continental! No, rub that – international! Step by step with the joyous come the unsettled. Languages roll off their lips from countries that have changed names so fast I can't keep up with them … Afghanistan, Zimbabwe, Iraq, Poland, Syria … ah, I remember Babylon and Ceylon, Siam…

In all the places in all the world … ah so much more to share; but think of this as a pointillist painting, these impressions of ordinary lives in a corner of England renowned for its light; like that white ship beyond – a shrine to light – Mr Turner. Here our communal spirits lift like those seabirds up there, clashing beaks with those pesky parakeets.

You know, I'm going to move over now, offer the last words to Toby the Bellman, this is the guy who carried the news on cobble and stone, from hoy to tavern, from front door to squares and gardens carrying the tale of the day. Nothing connecting with nothing? I think not.

> *Hear ye! Hear ye!*
> *We are not the only ones to walk this land and*
>   *watch this sea*
> *We are not the only ones to scratch a living praying*
>   *we eternal be*
> *Welcome the comers new and old who seek a life of*
>   *safety*
> *Welcome the creatures large and small who share*
>   *this isle like we*
> *Hear ye! Hear ye! This language ours so rich with*
>   *words*
> *Set by your emails and mobile phones and listen to*
>   *the birds.*

Acknowledgements

Maggie Harris gratefully acknowledges the support of a New Writing Award from Arts Council England.

Cultured Llama Publishing
Poems | Stories | Curious Things

Cultured Llama was born in a converted stable. This creature of humble birth drank greedily from the creative source of the poets, writers, artists and musicians that visited, and soon the llama fulfilled the destiny of its given name.

Cultured Llama is a publishing house, a multi-arts events promoter and a fundraiser for charity. It aspires to quality from the first creative thought through to the finished product.

www.culturedllama.co.uk

Also published by Cultured Llama

Poetry

strange fruits by Maria C. McCarthy
Paperback; 72pp; 203x127mm; 978-0-9568921-0-2; July 2011

A Radiance by Bethany W. Pope
Paperback; 70pp; 203x127mm; 978-0-9568921-3-3; June 2012

The Strangest Thankyou by Richard Thomas
Paperback; 98pp; 203x127mm; 978-0-9568921-5-7; October 2012

Unauthorised Person by Philip Kane
Paperback; 74pp; 203x127mm; 978-0-9568921-4-0; November 2012

The Night My Sister Went to Hollywood by Hilda Sheehan
Paperback; 82pp; 203x127mm; 978-0-9568921-8-8; March 2013

Notes from a Bright Field by Rose Cook
Paperback; 104pp; 203x127mm; 978-0-9568921-9-5; July 2013

Sounds of the Real World by Gordon Meade
Paperback; 104pp; 203x127 mm; 978-0-9926485-0-3; August 2013

Digging Up Paradise: Potatoes, People and Poetry in the Garden of England by Sarah Salway
Paperback; 160pp; 203x203 mm; 978-0-9926485-6-5; June 2014

The Fire in Me Now by Michael Curtis
Paperback; 98pp; 203x127 mm; 978-0-9926485-4-1; September 2014

Short of Breath by Vivien Jones
Paperback; 102pp; 203x127 mm; 978-0-9926485-5-8; November 2014

Cold Light of Morning by Julian Colton
Paperback; 90pp; 203x127mm; 978-0-9926485-7-2. March 2015

Short stories

Canterbury Tales on a Cockcrow Morning by Maggie Harris
Paperback; 136pp; 203x127mm; 978-0-9568921-6-4; September 2012

As Long as it Takes by Maria C. McCarthy
Paperback; 166pp; 203x127 mm; 978-0-9926485-1-0; February 2014

Anthologies: poetry and short stories

Unexplored Territory edited by Maria C. McCarthy
Paperback; 112pp; 203x127mm; 978-0-9568921-7-1; November 2012

Non-fiction

Punk Rock People Management: A No-Nonsense Guide to Hiring, Inspiring and Firing Staff by Peter Cook
Paperback; 38pp; 229x152mm; 978-0-9932119-0-4; March 2015

Do it Yourself: A History of Music in Medway by Stephen H. Morris
Paperback; 400pp; 229x152mm; 978-0-9926485-2-7; March 2015

The Music of Business: Business Excellence Fused with Music by Peter Cook
Paperback; 266pp; 210x148mm; 978-0-9932119-1-1; April 2015

Lightning Source UK Ltd.
Milton Keynes UK
UKOW02f0241010616

275346UK00001B/7/P